WALK THE BLUE FIELDS

Walk the Blue Fields

CLAIRE KEEGAN

BLACK CAT
a paperback original imprint of Grove /Atlantic, Inc.
New York

First published in 2007 by Faber and Faber Limited

Printed in the United States of America

First Grove Atlantic paperback edition: July 2008

ISBN 978-0-8021-7049-1
eISBN 978-0-8021-8972-1

Library of Congress Cataloging-in-Publication data is available for this title.

Black Cat
an imprint of Grove Atlantic
154 West 14th Street
New York, NY 10011

Distributed by Publishers Group West

groveatlantic.com

23 24 25 26   11 10

For Jim and Claire

The Parting Gift

When sunlight reaches the foot of the dressing table, you get up and look through the suitcase again. It's hot in New York but it may turn cold in winter. All morning the bantam cocks have crowed. It's not something you will miss. You must dress and wash, polish your shoes. Outside, dew lies on the fields, white and blank as pages. Soon the sun will burn it off. It's a fine day for the hay.

In her bedroom your mother is moving things around, opening and closing doors. You wonder what it will be like for her when you leave. Part of you doesn't care. She talks through the door.

'You'll have a boiled egg?'

'No thanks, Ma.'

'You'll have something?'

'Later on, maybe.'

'I'll put one on for you.'

Downstairs, water runs into the kettle, the bolt slides back. You hear the dogs rush in, the shutters folding. You've always preferred this house in summer: cool feeling in the kitchen, the back door open, scent of the dark wallflowers after rain.

In the bathroom you brush your teeth. The screws in the mirror have rusted, and the glass is cloudy. You look at yourself and know you have failed the Leaving Cert. The last exam was history and you blanked out on the dates. You confused the methods of warfare, the kings. English was worse. You tried to explain that line about the dancer

3

and the dance.

You go back to the bedroom and take out the passport. You look strange in the photograph, lost. The ticket says you will arrive in Kennedy Airport at 12.25, much the same time as you leave. You take one last look around the room: walls papered yellow with roses, high ceiling stained where the slate came off, cord of the electric heater swinging out like a tail from under the bed. It used to be an open room at the top of the stairs but Eugene put an end to all of that, got the carpenters in and the partition built, installed the door. You remember him giving you the key, how much that meant to you at the time.

Downstairs, your mother stands over the gas cooker waiting for the pot to boil. You stand at the door and look out. It hasn't rained for days; the spout that runs down from the yard is little more than a trickle. The scent of hay drifts up from neighbouring fields. As soon as the dew burns it off, the Rudd brothers will be out in the meadows turning the rows, saving it while the weather lasts. With pitchforks they'll gather what the baler leaves behind. Mrs Rudd will bring out the flask, the salad. They will lean against the bales and eat their fill. Laughter will carry up the avenue, clear, like birdcall over water.

'It's another fine day.' You feel the need for speech.

Your mother makes some animal sound in her throat. You turn to look at her. She wipes her eyes with the back of her hand. She's never made any allowance for tears.

'Is Eugene up?' she says.

'I don't know. I didn't hear him.'

'I'll go and wake him.'

It's going on for six. Still an hour before you leave. The saucepan boils and you go over to lower the flame. Inside, three eggs knock against each other. One is cracked, a rib-

4

bon streaming white. You turn down the gas. You don't like yours soft.

Eugene comes down wearing his Sunday clothes. He looks tired. He looks much the same as he always does.

'Well, Sis,' he says. 'Are you all set?'

'Yeah.'

'You have your ticket and everything?'

'I do.'

Your mother puts out the cups and plates, slices a quarter out of the loaf. This knife is old, its teeth worn in places. You eat the bread, drink the tea and wonder what Americans eat for breakfast. Eugene tops his egg, butters bread, shares it with the dogs. Nobody says anything. When the clock strikes six, Eugene reaches for his cap.

'There's a couple of things I've to do up the yard,' he says. 'I won't be long.'

'That's all right.'

'You'd want to leave on time,' your mother says. 'You wouldn't want to get a puncture.'

You place your dirty dishes on the draining board. You have nothing to say to your mother. If you started, you would say the wrong things and you wouldn't want it to end that way. You go upstairs but you'd rather not go back into the room. You stand on the landing. They start talking in the kitchen but you don't hear what they say. A sparrow swoops down onto the window ledge and pecks at his reflection, his beak striking the glass. You watch him until you can't watch him any longer and he flies away.

❧

Your mother didn't want a big family. Sometimes, when she lost her temper, she told you she would put you in a bucket and drown you. As a child you imagined being taken by force to the edge of the Slaney River, being placed in a bucket, and the bucket being flung out from the bank, floating for a while before it sank. As you grew older you knew it was only a figure of speech, and then you believed it was just an awful thing to say. People sometimes said awful things.

Your eldest sister was sent off to the finest boarding school in Ireland, and became a school teacher. Eugene was gifted in school but when he turned fourteen your father pulled him out to work the land. In the photographs the eldest are dressed up: satin ribbons and short trousers, a blinding sun in their eyes. The others just came along, as nature took its course, were fed and clothed, sent off to the boarding schools. Sometimes they came back for a bank-holiday weekend. They brought gifts and an optimism that quickly waned. You could see them remembering everything, the existence, turning rigid when your father's shadow crossed the floor. Leaving, they'd feel cured, impatient to get away.

Your turn at boarding school never came. By then your father saw no point in educating girls; you'd go off and another man would have the benefit of your education. If you were sent to the day school you could help in the house, the yard. Your father moved into the other room but your mother gave him sex on his birthday. She'd go into his room and they'd have it there. It never took long and they never made noise but you knew. And then that too stopped and you were sent instead, to sleep with your father. It happened once a month or so, and always when Eugene was out.

You went willingly at first, crossed the landing in your nightdress, put your head on his arm. He played with you,

6

praised you, told you you had the brains, that you were the brightest child. Then the terrible hand reachs down under the clothes to pull up the nightdress, the fingers, strong from milking, finding you. The other hand hand going at himself until he groaned and then him asking you to reach over for the cloth, saying you could go then, if you wanted. The mandatory kiss at the end, stubble, and cigarettes on the breath. Sometimes he gave you a cigarette of your own and you could lie beside him smoking, pretending you were someone else. You'd go into the bathroom when it was over and wash, telling yourself it meant nothing, hoping the water would be hot.

Now you stand on the landing trying to remember happiness, a good day, an evening, a kind word. It seems apt to search for something happy to make the parting harder but nothing comes to mind. Instead you remember that time the setter had all those pups. It was around the same time your mother started sending you into his room. In the spout-house, your mother leant over the half barrel, and held the sack under the water until the whimpering stopped and the sack went still. That day she drowned the pups, she turned her head and looked at you, and smiled.

Eugene comes up and finds you standing there.

'It doesn't matter,' he says. 'Pay no heed.'

'What doesn't matter?'

He shrugs and goes into the room he shares with your father. You drag the suitcase downstairs. Your mother hasn't washed the dishes. She is standing there at the door with a bottle of holy water. She shakes some of this water on you.

7

Some of it gets in your eyes. Eugene comes down with the car keys.

'Da wants to talk to you.'

'He's not getting up?'

'No. You're to go up to him.'

'Go on,' Ma says. 'Don't leave empty-handed.'

You go back up the stairs, stop outside his room. You haven't gone through this door since the blood started, since you were twelve. You open it. It's dim inside, stripes of summer light around the curtains. There's that same old smell of cigarette smoke and feet. You look at his shoes and socks beside the bed. You feel sick. He sits up in his vest, the cattle dealer's eyes taking it all in, measuring.

'So you're going to America,' he says.

You say you are.

'Aren't you the sly one?' He folds the sheet over his belly. 'Will it be warm out there?'

You say it will.

'Will there be anyone to meet you?'

'Yes.' Agree with him. Always, that was your strategy.

'That's all right, so.'

You wait for him to get the wallet out or to tell you where it is, to fetch it. Instead, he puts his hand out. You don't want to touch him but maybe the money is in his hand. In desperation you extend yours, and he shakes it. He draws you towards him. He wants to kiss you. You don't have to look at him to know he's smiling. You pull away, turn out of the room but he calls you back. This is his way. He'll give it to you now that he knows you thought you'd get nothing.

'And another thing,' he says. 'Tell Eugene I want them meadows knocked by dark.'

You go out and close the door. In the bathroom you

wash your hands, your face, compose yourself once more.

'I hope he gave you money?' your mother says.

'He did,' you say.

'How much did he give you?'

'A hundred pound.'

'His own daughter, the last of ye, and he wouldn't even get out of the bed and you going to America, " she says. "Wasn't it a black bastard I married!'

'Are you ready?' Eugene says. 'We better hit the road.'

You put your arms around your mother. You don't know why. She changes when you do this. You can feel her getting soft in your arms.

'I'll send word, Ma, when I get there.'

'Do,' she says.

'It'll be night before I do.'

'I know,' she says. 'The journey's long.'

Eugene takes the suitcase and you follow him outside. The cherry trees are bending. *The stronger the wind, the stronger the tree.* The sheep dogs follow you. You walk on, past the flower beds, the pear trees, on out towards the car. The Cortina is parked under the chestnut's shade. You can smell the wild mint beside the diesel tank. Eugene turns the engine and tries to make some joke, starts down the avenue. You look again at your handbag, your ticket, the passport. You will get there, you tell yourself. They will meet you.

Eugene stops in the avenue before the gates.

'Da gave you nothing, sure he didn't?'

'What?'

'I know he didn't. You needn't let on.'

'It doesn't matter.'

'All I have is a twenty-pound note. I can send you money later on.'

9

'It doesn't matter.'

'Do you think it would be safe to send money in the post?'

It is a startling question, stupid. You look at the gates, at the woods beyond.

'Safe?'

'Yeah.'

'Yes,' you say you think it will.

You get out and open the gates. He drives through, stops to wait for you. As you put the wire on, the filly trots down to the edge of the field, leans up against the fence, and whinnies. She's a red chestnut with one white stocking. You sold her to buy your ticket but she will not be collected until tomorrow. That was the arrangement. You watch her and turn away but it's impossible not to look back. Your eyes follow the gravel road, the strip of green between the tracks, on up to the granite arch left there from Protestant days and, past it, your mother who has come out to see the last of you. She waves a cowardly little wave, and you wonder if she will ever forgive you for leaving her there with her husband.

On down the avenue, the Rudds are already in the meadows. There's a shot from an engine as something starts, a bright clap of laughter. You pass Barna Cross where you used to catch the bus to the Community School. Towards the end, you hardly bothered going. You simply sat in the wood under the trees all day or, if it was raining, you found a hayshed. Sometimes you read the books your sisters left behind. Sometimes you fell asleep. Once a man came into his hayshed and found you there. You kept your eyes closed. He stood there for a long time and then he went away.

'There's something you should know,' Eugene says.

'Oh?'

'I'm not staying.'

'What do you mean?'

'I'm giving up the land. They can keep it.'

'What?'

'Can you see me living there with them until the end of their days? Could you see me bringing a woman in? What woman could stand it? I'd have no life.'

'But what about all the work you've done, all that time?'

'I don't care about any of that,' he says. 'All that is over.'

'Where will you go?'

'I don't know. I'll rent some place.'

'Where?'

'I don't know yet. I was waiting until you left. I didn't think any further.'

'You didn't stay on my account?'

He slows the car and looks over. 'I did,' he says. 'But I wasn't much use, was I, Sis?'

It is the first time anyone has ever mentioned it. It feels like a terrible thing, being said.

'You couldn't be there all the time.'

'No,' he says. 'I suppose I couldn't.'

Between Baltinglass and Blessington the road winds. You remember this part of the road. You came this way for the All Ireland finals. Your father had a sister in Tallaght he could stay with, a hard woman who made great tarts and left a chain of smoke. Boggy fields, bad land surround this road, and a few ponies grazing. As a child, you thought this was the West of Ireland. It used to make the adults laugh, to hear you say it. And now you suddenly remember one good thing about your father. It was before you had begun to go into his room. He had gone into the village and stopped at the garage for petrol. The girl at the pumps came up to him and told him she was the brightest girl in the class, the best at every subject, until you came along. He'd come back from the village and repeated this, and he was proud because you were brighter than the Protestant's daughter.

Close to the airport, planes appear in the sky. Eugene parks the car and helps you find the desk. Neither one of you knows exactly what to do. They look at your passport, take your suitcase and tell you where to go. You step onto moving stairs that frighten you. There's a coffee shop where Eugene tries to make you eat a fry but you don't want to eat or stay and keep him company.

Your brother embraces you. You have never been embraced this way. When his stubble grazes your face, you pull back.

'I'm sorry,' he says.

'It's all right.'

'Goodbye, Sis.'

'Goodbye, Eugene. Take care.'

'Watch out for pickpockets in New York.'

You cannot answer.

'Write,' he says quickly. 'Don't forget to write.'

'I won't. Don't worry.'

You follow passengers through a queue and leave him behind. He will not go back for the fry; he hasn't the time. You did not have to deliver the message. You know he will put his boot down, be home before noon, have the meadows knocked long before dark. After that there will be corn to cut. Already the winter barley's turning. September will bring more work, old duties to the land. Sheds to clean out, cattle to test, lime to spread, dung. You know he will never leave the fields.

A stranger asks for your handbag, and you give it to

him. You pass through a frame that has no door and your handbag is returned to you. On the other side, the lights are bright. There's the smell of perfume and roasted coffee beans, expensive things. You make out bottles of tanning lotion, a rack of dark glasses. It is all getting hazy but you keep on going, because you must, past the T-shirts and the duty-free towards the gate. When you find it, there is hardly anyone there but you know this is the place. You look for another door, make out part of a woman's body. You push it, and it opens. You pass bright hand-basins, mirrors. Someone asks are you all right – *such a stupid question* – but you do not cry until you have opened and closed another door, until you have safely locked yourself inside your stall.

Walk the Blue Fields

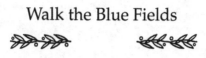

Earlier, the women came with flowers, each one a deeper shade of red. In the chapel, where they waited, their scent was strong. The organist slowly played the Bach toccata once again but a thrill of doubt was spreading through the pews. Already the slant of morning sun had crossed the granite ridge of the baptismal and slid into the font. The priest lifted his head and stared at the open doors where the bridesmaids, in green silk, stood silent. Beyond them, a pale cloud was splitting in the April sky. It was torn and had begun to drift before John Lawlor came up the steps with his only child and gave her away.

Without any reference to time, the priest welcomed everyone and went on to perform the ceremony. There was a moment when he stumbled over the words but, before long, the vows were made and Jackson had the plain gold ring on her finger. In the vestry, the priest noticed how the bride's hand shook as she lifted the heavy fountain pen, how sparingly the dark ink flowed onto the register but Jackson's bold strokes clearly signi-fied his name.

Now, the priest stands outside and stares at the chapel grounds. It is a fresh day, bright with wind. Confetti has blown across the tombstones, the paving, up the grave-yard path. On the yew, a scrap of veil quivers. He reaches up and takes it from the branch. It feels stiff in his hand, stranger than cloth. He would like, now, to change his clothes and head for the country road, to cross the stile and walk down to the river. There, in the marshy patch between the fields, his presence would make the wild ducks scatter. Further down, at the edge of the river, he would feel calm but as soon as he turns the key in the chapel door, he faces up the street where his duty lies.

Many of the shops in the village today are closed: scrubbed steel trays lie empty in the butcher's window; blinds sit tight behind the draper's pane. Only the newsagent's door is open, a girl with scissors shearing the heads off yesterday's papers. The priest crosses the street and walks up the avenue to the hotel. This was once the Protestant's estate. On either side, the trees are tall and here the wind is strangely human. A tender speech is combing through the willows. In a bare whisper, the elms lean. Something about the place conjures up the ancient past: the hound, the spear, the spinning wheel. There's pleasure to be had in history. What's recent is another matter and painful to recall.

Out on the lawn, the bride and groom with relatives are gathered. The bridesmaids, in their blustering gowns, are laughing now at something the best man has said. The photographer is out front, telling them where and how to stand. The priest crosses the red carpet and reaches out to shake the groom's hand once again. He's a low-set man with common blue eyes and a great deal of strength in his body.

'I wish you all the best,' says the priest. 'I hope you will be very happy.'

'Thank you, Father. Won't you step in and get your photo taken with the rest of us?' he says, placing him beside the bride.

The bride is a beauty whose freckled shoulders, in this dress, are bare. A long string of pearls lies heavy against her skin. The priest steps in close without touching her and stares at the line of her scalp where the shining red hair is parted. She looks calm but the bouquet in her hand is trembling.

'You must be cold,' he says.

'I'm not.'

'You must be.'

'I'm not,' she says. 'I feel nothing.'

Finally, she looks at him. The green eyes are stony and give nothing away.

'Look this way, please!'

The priest looks over the photographer's head, at the clouds. The clouds are moving fast, obscuring the sun, throwing legitimate shadows on the lawn.

'Lovely! Hold that.' The formation stiffens while a button is pressed, then falls apart. 'Could we have the groom's family now? Would all members of the groom's family please step forward!'

Inside the hotel there's the mordant heat of the crowd, the spill of guests. A waitress near the front desk is ladling punch. Another stands with a sharp knife, slicing a long, smoked salmon. The guests are queuing up, reaching for forks, capers, cuts of lemon. All about them, there are flowers. Never has the priest seen such flowers: wide-open tulips, blue hyacinths, trumpeting gladioli. He stands beside a crystal jug of roses and breathes in. Their scent is heavy. The need for a drink comes over him and he faces into the bar.

'Hello, Father,' says Miss Dunne, a stout woman in a multicoloured dress. 'That was a decent ceremony. Short and sweet, you kept it.'

'That's the easy bit, Miss Dunne. I hope they will be happy now.'

'Only time will tell,' she says. 'You could be jumping the gun.'

The priest smiles. 'Will you take a drink?'

'No,' she says. 'I never touch it.' Her arms are folded.

'Never?'

'No. Never. If you don't know why, just stay till evening.'

'You'll have a mineral water?'

'I won't,' she says. 'I'll wait for me dinner.'

The priest realises she is happy standing there on her own. He goes to the bar and orders a hot whiskey. The barmaid sighs and puts the kettle on, stabs a slice of lemon with cloves, drops a spoon into an empty glass. He looks at the crowd and waits for someone to descend. Mostly it's women who talk to him. There are people here who would like to talk. There are others who owe him money.

Mrs Jackson, the groom's mother, comes in from the cold. Her colour is high, clashing with the lilac dress. She takes her hat off and, not knowing where to place it, puts it on again.

'Where was I going wud this?' she says. 'An auld woman like me.'

It's the old game he used to love and has tired of: they put themselves down so he can easily raise them up again. Always looking for the compliment.

'Would you stop,' he says. 'Don't you look marvellous.'

'God help us, Father, but it's little you know,' she says, standing an inch taller.

'Easy knowing you're a priest,' says her niece. 'A man would never say that.' She is studying the room, clearly disappointed in the men that are there.

Mrs Jackson dismisses the remark. 'Well, at least that much is done. I have only the one left now and, God knows, I could be left with him till the end of my days.'

'You don't think he'll marry?'

'Who'd take him? A bloody nuisance, he is. All work and all play. Nothing in between.'

'You'll take a drink, Mrs Jackson?'

'I won't,' she says. 'I'll go off and see about this dinner, in the name of God.'

A young woman from outside the parish leans over the bar, trying to get service. She leans over the barber who is staring at his glass.

'Is that glass half full or half empty would you say, Father?'

'It's whatever you think,' the priest says.

'Well, I don't know what else you've been drinking,' the woman says, 'but surely it can't be one without being the other.'

The barber frowns and then its meaning registers.

'Women,' he says, shaking his head. 'The women always have an answer.'

A flower girl races past, trailing more children. The hot whiskey settles him, reminds him of winter nights in his youth. He begins to think of Christmas and his mother, how she poured the stout into the pudding and made him stir it, made him wish. She had encouraged without pushing him towards the priesthood. Once, as an altar boy, he'd stood in the vestry and let his hand trail over the cassock, the surplice. Winter light was staining itself on the high window and in the chapel the choir was practising 'How Great Thou Art'. He had, at that moment, felt the path opening, but there is no time to dwell on such things here. Lawlor, the bride's father, has stepped in tight and clasped his hand. In his palm, the priest feels money.

'Something for your trouble,' Lawlor says quietly.

'Thank you,' the priest accepts. 'It was my pleasure.'

Lawlor is a widower with two hundred acres on the

Carlow road. The silk tie is perfectly knotted, its stripe bringing up the dark red thread in the suit. He is well known as a man of taste, well liked. He looks across the bar at the groom who has his head down, listening to something another man is saying.

'Do you think that brother of his will be fit to stand?' Lawlor asks.

'Won't the dinner soon be served?' says the priest.

'We've arranged it so we won't be hanging around. They should be calling us any minute now.' He turns silent and stares again at the groom. 'When a woman makes up her mind, you can't stand in her way. You are best out of it.'

'Things have their own way of sorting themselves out,' the priest consoles.

'Some do,' he says, dropping his head, toeing the stool with the big, polished shoe. 'You have to stand back and let them at it, let them make their own mistakes. That's the trouble. And if you don't go to that trouble, you ask for more.'

The girl who was ladling punch comes into the bar with a gong. 'Please take your seats! Ladies and gentlemen! Dinner will be served!'

There's a ripple of surprise. Women reach for their handbags. Drinkers panic and order another round. A trickle flows towards the ballroom where the tables have been set.

'You know where I am,' says the priest. 'If ever you need me.'

'I hope I won't have to call on you,' Lawlor says.

'Call anyhow,' the priest says. 'I'm home most evenings.'

In the Gents, he stands before the mirror and washes his hands, combs the hair back off his forehead. It is growing fast, falling down over his eyes but the last time he went to the barber, he was given a rough cut. Donal Jackson, the best man, comes in, leans against the wall, and urinates. The stream is long and noisy on the tile. He turns before his cock is put away. It is a huge cock and he has difficulty getting it back into the rented trousers.

'A fucken ornament, Father,' he says. 'Much like your own.'

'Aisy!' shouts Kennedy, who has flushed and come out of the stall. 'There's no need for that. Would you ever put that thing away!' He is half amused. 'Don't mind this blackguard, Father. Pay no heed.'

Going out the door, the priest hears laughter. There was a time, not too long ago, when they would have waited until he could not have heard. He must go to the bar and compose himself once more. Weddings are hard. The drink flows and the words come out and he has to be there. A man loses his daughter to a younger man. A woman sees her son throwing himself away on a lesser woman. It is something they half believe. There's the expense, the sentiment, the no going back. Any time promises are made in public, people cry.

He stands at the counter and orders a small Powers. When the barmaid hands it to him, she says it's paid for. The priest looks up. At the far counter, holding a fresh pint of stout, stands the groom. He raises his glass and smiles. The priest lifts the whiskey and takes a sip. It had never occurred to him, until now, that Jackson might have known.

The crowd has filled the ballroom, covered now with tables laid. There's the flash of silverware, candle flame, the grate of chairs on polished wood. Half the parish is here; a small wedding will no longer do. At the head table,

23

every seat but the groom's is taken. Why had he assumed that a chair would be reserved up there for him? Awkwardly, he does the round of tables, looking for his name. Miss Dunne signals, points. He's been seated at a table with relatives. On his left, the bride's uncle. To his right, the groom's aunt.

'I see they've put you down with the rest of the sinners,' says the aunt.

The priest offers no response. They milk the subject of the weather for a minute or two then look at the menu. The courses are printed in gold, and they are given a choice: cream of vegetable soup to start or crab meat in an avocado pear. Then poached salmon with parsley sauce or lamb in a rosemary jus.

The groom's aunt sees no need for all the fuss.

'Wouldn't a piece of boiled ham do us? It's far from alvocadoes we were reared,' she says, looking for praise.

'I wonder where they poached the salmon?' Sinnott says. 'I hope it wasn't my part of the river.' He is a wiry man who seldom pays his dues and has confessed to stealing sheep off Jackson's hill.

Lawlor, at the head table, taps a glass and the crowd turns silent. A member of staff comes over with a microphone and hands it to the priest. Mechanically, he begins.

'Bless us, O Lord, and these Thy gifts . . .'

Heads bow. A crying child is taken from the room. As soon as he reaches the Amen, platters of avocado pears and bowls of soup appear. Bread rolls are buttered. Heads dip. Girls with a bottle in each hand pour red and white wine. Dishes of roast potatoes are brought out, vegetables, boats of gravy. Comfort is taken in the food and silence presides until the first wave of hunger is satiated. Then the talk begins.

'You never put on an ounce, Father,' the aunt says. 'Don't mind me asking but how do keep the weight down?'

'I walk,' he says, letting out a sigh.

'The walking is great, they say. Do you go far?'

'I go out the road as far as the creamery and on down to the river,' he says. 'I go any day I'm able.'

'I know that way,' Miss Dunne says. 'Were you ever down wud the Chinaman, Father?'

'No.' He laughs. 'What Chinaman?'

'Well, you wouldn't know him – he's not a Christian – but there's people goes down to him for the cure.'

'The cure?'

'Aye,' she says, reaching for the salt.

'Where, exactly, does he live?'

'Down below Redmond's in the caravan. You know there at the back of the hay shed? You must know it if you do be down that way.'

'He's a refugee, some relation of them people wud the Chinese,' the Jackson man says. 'Redmond of the quarry hired him as a labourer and now he's down there tending the ewes.'

'Says he hasn't lost a lamb yet,' Breen says. 'They say, in all fairness, that he's a good man even though he doesn't always do it our way.'

'He won't have a dog. Has some terror of dogs,' says Mike Brennan from the hill.

'He'd probably ate the bloody sheep dog,' Sinnott says, stretching out for the last roast potato.

'What, exactly, does he do?' the priest asks.

'He's shepherding, didn't I say?' says Miss Dunne.

'No. I mean, what cure does he have?'

'I don't rightly know, Father. All I know is there's people goes to him. I never go near him. If an'thing's ailing me, I go to Nail the bone-setter.'

'A great man if you've a dish out in yer back,' says Breen 'Only you could be behind a greyhound.'

'Or a fecking pony!' says Sinnott. 'I had to wait two hour after a lame piebald.'

There is laughter.

'If you've an'thing ailing you, the Chinaman's the man.'

'It's all talk. Sure what use could he be? Hasn't a word of English. There'd be no way of telling him what's ailing ya.'

'Well, there'd be nothing to stop you telling him!' Mike Brennan laughs.

'You could point!' says Miss Dunne.

'You could drop your drawers, tell him which end of the parish you were reared in, and hope for the best,' says Sinnott. 'Sure he's a Chink: ates dog and shites tay!'

'Aisy!' says Brennan with a frown. 'There's a man of the cloth here.'

'Aye,' says Sinnott with a grunt. 'And we all know the white cloth is aisy stained.'

The laughter tumbles quickly into a fragile silence. Breen coughs. The aunt straightens her knife and fork once more.

'It's much you'd know about stains,' says Miss Dunne, 'and you wud five sisters ironing every crease out of your pyjamas.'

It's a fair attempt at a rescue but Sinnott's remark smoulders. The priest cuts into the lamb. Mike Brennan looks across the room where another man is making his way across the floor on crutches.

'Speaking of bones,' he says, 'what happened to Donoghue?'

'Got a kick of a heifer this morning,' says Sinnott.

'That'll learn him to warm his hands. Was he wud the doctor?'

'No. He wouldn't go.'

'You couldn't get him to go,' says Breen.

'He must have had the sticks, so. Two things you should never keep in a house: crutches – and a pram.'

'There's the voice of experience!' cries Miss Dunne.

'Yez can laugh away but there was never a truer word. When Mary was in having the last, I took the pram up the yard and gave it the torch,' says Brennan. 'She ate me when she came home but wasn't it nearly time? Sure the hens took to laying out in the Moses basket.'

'Is it seven you have, or eight?' says the aunt.

'I've nine,' says Brennan, searching his pockets for cigarettes. 'And isn't it a terrible thing, after all that, to have to go outside for a fag?'

Now that the main course is over, the anxiety of service dies down. The girls who come out to remove their dinner plates are different girls. Nothing's been broken. No one has gone without. The desserts come out: almond tart with strawberries, sherry trifle, cream. They are just about to lift their spoons and pitch the next round of speech when Donal Jackson, at the head table, strikes his glass and stands. As soon as he stands, he falls back into his chair. The crowd turns towards him, falls silent. Ears prick. A titter falls loose in the room. The best man tries, again, to get to his feet. This time he manages to stand but he has to lean on the table, his hand flat on the cloth.

'Hello everybody!' he cries out. 'Hello!'

The groom mumbles something about keeping the bastarding thing short. It is heard, without meaning to be heard, over the microphone.

'Good day to yous all!' the best man cries. 'I hope ye've had your fill.'

He stops at this point, unsure of how to go on. He looks

27

down at the bride. He looks at his brother.

'When my brother started courting Kate here, we all said he'd never pull as fine a bird.' He looks at the tablecloth, the glasses, the silver salt and pepper shakers. 'Now that we seen he's done it, the only pity is she doesn't have a sister!' He pushes the tablecloth and the dishes move. A glass of red wine tips over staining the white linen.

Sinnott looks hard at the priest and smiles, looks back at the best man.

'If she had a sister we could have shared the land and –'

Lawlor quickly takes the microphone from his hand. He does so with all the grace of the gentleman he is and begins to thank everyone, most sincerely, for coming. He says he is glad that his only daughter has found a good husband. He says he did his best to raise her well and, although her mother cannot be here, he knows she is looking down on them and blessing this day. He praises the food, the wine, the service. He thanks the priest for the simple ceremony, the bridesmaids who bore witness, and all the groom's people. He welcomes the groom to the family, and hopes he will treat his daughter well for the rest of her life. He can hope for nothing more, he says, and sits down.

The groom unfolds a piece of paper and thanks everyone again, in turn, mirroring his father-in-law's speech. The bride sits quietly, surrounded by all the men making speeches. A waitress comes round with champagne but she wants none of it. As she sits there, with her hand caressing the stem of her glass, the priest remembers something. It is a clear, resurrected memory that makes him wish he was alone.

Applause rises when the cake comes out. The bride and groom stand and take hold of the knife. The blade is sunk deep into the bottom tier and the obligatory photograph is taken. Soon after, the cake comes back, cut up on tiny plates, dusted with sugar. Tea is poured, coffee.

Miss Lawlor reaches out and stuffs a serviette into her handbag.

'A souvenir,' she says. 'I must have a dozen now.'

Again, the priest is handed the microphone. He stands up and says grace without feeling any of the words. Lately, when he has prayed, his prayers have not been answered. Where is God? he has asked. Not, what is God? He does not mind not knowing God. His faith has not faltered – that's what's strange – but he wishes God would show himself. All he wants is a sign. Some nights he gets down on his knees when the housekeeper is gone and the curtains are pulled tight across the windows and prays to God to show him how to be a priest.

Everyone is asked to finish so the tables can be pushed back, the space cleared for dancing. People abandon the ballroom for the bar, the toilets, go out to the beer garden to smoke. At this point, the priest could leave. He could go up to those still sober enough to remember he said goodbye, and shake their hands. In his house, he knows a fire is set. All he has to do is go back and set a match to it. Sleep would tug at him and the day would end. But he must stay for the dance. He will stay to see the dance, then he will go.

The music begins with a slow waltz. 'Could I Have this Dance for the Rest of My Life?' As the groom is leading his bride onto the floor, the hem of her dress snags on the heel of her shoe. She stoops to fix it, blushing. She has taken off the veil so the back of her neck is naked, but for the pearls. When she straightens up, Jackson takes her in his arms. Willingly she seems to go. Lights catch the diamond in her engagement ring. The white shoes follow the course her husband makes around the floor. They circle once, and once again, and then his brother comes out with the maid of honour. He seems light on his feet. The best man may be incapable of speech, but he can dance. The groomsman follows with his bridesmaid. They seem shy, unsure of themselves, of each other. After three waltzes, the music stops and the best man asks his brother if he can dance with the bride. The groom looks at him. Lawlor is standing at the edge of the dance-floor trying to catch the groom's eye. He will have difficulty, the priest realises, staying out of this, even though he said he must. The groom hesitates but he consents and soon the maid of honour is exchanged for the bride.

The band picks up the pace, changing to a quickstep. The best man begins the jive. Years back, he won some type of jiving competition, and now he is determined to show his skill. He makes an arch of his arm, and the bride passes under, comes out behind him but she is not moving fast enough for his liking. He pushes the bride into a spin, but when he turns, to spin off her, his hand does not catch hers; instead it catches the string of pearls and when he spins, the string breaks.

The priest freezes as the pearls slip off the string. He watches how they hop off the polished floor. One pearl hits the skirting board, rolls back past Miss Dunne's outstretched hand. She lets out a sigh as it rolls back towards the priest's chair. He puts his hand down and lifts it. It is warm in his hand, warm from her. This, more than anything else in the day, startles him.

The priest walks across the dance floor. The bride is standing there with her hands out. When he places the pearl in her hand, she looks into his eyes. There are tears there but she is too proud to blink and let one fall. If she blinked, he would take her hand and take her away from this place. This, at least, is what he tells himself. It's what she once wanted but two people hardly ever want the same thing at any given point in life. It is sometimes the hardest part of being human.

'I am so sorry,' he says.

He looks at her open palms, at the pearls accumulating. He lifts his eyes back to her face. Lawlor is staring at him but Breen comes up and breaks it.

'How many had you?' Breen says.

'How many?' says the bride, shaking her head.

'Aye,' he says. 'Have you any notion how many was on the string?' Breen looks at her and changes. 'Ah, don't be crying, girl. Tis only a string. Tis aisy mended.'

Down at the ballroom door, the groom has caught the best man by the collar. The big hand is tight, the face white in temper.

'You mad bollocks!' he roars. 'Could you not control yourself for the one fucken day!'

Lovely to be out in the avenue again, to leave that terrible music behind. The wind has died and now the trees are still. On a bough, a crow sits watchful. Down the street, a chimney throws white smoke against the sky. The newsagent has closed her door but in the betting shop, a TV light still flickers. The priest pauses at the window, sees there a girl, fast asleep with an open book. He would like to go in and wake her, to tell her that she will get a crick in her neck but he walks on down to the parish house. As soon as his foot touches the deep gravel, he knows he cannot go inside. He turns back down the street, past the petrol pumps, and heads out the country road.

So, she is married. For a moment, he feels the possibility of all things new and then it vanishes. He passes the high walls of the convent, then the tubular steel fence of the mart. There's no pavement now, just the bare road, a fringe of dead leaves under his feet. It is slippery, in places, and he tells himself he does not really know where he is going. He passes Jackson's gate, the milk cartons left standing in the crate. Every now and then a beast in some field or shed lets out a roar. Many of the cattle in this parish will not be fed tonight. He walks without allowing any single thought to dominate his mind. After a few miles he can hear, under the road, the comforting noise of the river.

When he reaches the creamery, he turns down Hunter's Lane. Here, the Blackstairs tower over the land, throwing the fields into strange, blue shadow. Hunting men come down here on Sundays, after mass. They've left dead fowl at the house: cock pheasants, ducks, a goose. The house-keeper has hung them, plucked them, served them up on the dinner table. The priest doesn't like to think of this even though he's taken pleasure in the meals, the gravy.

The lane ends where a house once stood, its gabled walls choked in ivy. At the marshy patch where the alders grow, there's panic on the water, a flutter, and the wild ducks rise. The catkins shiver after them. The priest stops still and looks at the sky for the heron. Never once has he come this way without seeing her. It is asking much to see her again but suddenly she's there, her slow wings carrying her in a placid curve against the sky.

Down at the river, the sleepy brown water runs on. The peace is deeper as always simply because it's still there. On the water's surface, the reflection of the far bank's trees is corrugated. A single cloud floats on the sky, so pale and out of place, like a cloud left over from another day. He remembers the snatch of bridal veil on the yews, puts his hand in his pocket and feels it there. He takes it out, lets it fall. Before it touches the water, he regrets it but he had his chance, and now his chance is gone.

There was a milky fog in the orchard the night she came up to the house. It was All Soul's, and he was alone in the parlour with the fire blazing. Earlier that day he'd given last rites to a young man at the hospital, then he'd driven back to say evening Mass. It was one of those nights when he felt the impossibility of being alone. He was thinking of the young man, of how he himself was still young. The clock on the mantelpiece was loud. He threw more coal on the fire and paced the floor. She came to get a Mass card signed, for her mother. He asked her to come in, to sit with him. She had stayed, he felt, so as not to offend him. He never meant to touch her but when she stared into the fire, the priest looked at the line on her scalp where the dark red hair was parted. He'd reached out simply to feel the heat of the fire on her hair. That was all he had meant to do but she had misunderstood the gesture.

Always, they met in out-of-the-way places: on the rough strand at Cahore or Blackwater, in the woods beyond the common paths of Avondale. Once, they ran into Miss Dunne on the strand. She was walking towards them and it was too late to turn away but just as they were about to meet, she turned towards the sea. She had not on that day nor ever since given any hint that she had seen them.

The seasons passed and winter came again. They got away, travelled north to The Silent Valley and stayed in a little guest-house near Newry town. That night, over dinner, she caressed the stem of her glass and told him she couldn't stand it any longer. If he could not leave the priesthood, she would not see him this way again. They had gone to a heritage park the next morning on the way home, walked backwards through the ages, from Viking yard and house through the crannógs, and wound up at a Neolithic tomb. There, they had stood at the edge of an artificial lake where a crude, wooden boat was half submerged. The water's surface was thick with dandelion seed. A cold breeze hissed through the reeds but they were silent, locked in the knowledge that nothing again would ever be the same.

Now, she is married. Tonight, Jackson will lead her to a room and take her dress off. The priest can still see the brother's cock, the size of it, how he couldn't get it back into his trousers. He leans over the bank of the river, pulls the heads off a few tall weeds. He should go back to town, get into his bed, but he is unwilling to let the day end. Instead, he walks in the opposite direction, crossing the stiles between the fields. The land changes from coarse stubble ground to bright shoots of wheat. Such a dry winter as they had. Further on, there's smooth pasture and, all about him, sheep are grazing. So, this is Redmond's land. He looks up towards the road, sees there the roof of the big hayshed and beside it, standing in the shelter, a caravan.

As soon as he sees it, he tells himself he did not come down here for this. The last thing he wants is company but his feet seem, of their own accord, to take him through the pasture. In a sheltered place, beyond currant bushes, a patch of ground is neatly fenced with wooden posts and sheep wire. Drills are set in neat rows, fresh clay on a rake. When he pushes the plain timber gate, it squeals. The priest stands there in the garden for a while, listening. He hears nothing from inside and, feeling confident that nobody is home, knocks on the door. As soon as he knocks, he turns to leave but the door opens and a Chinaman, wearing flip-flops and a loose track-suit is standing there.

'Yes,' he smiles. 'Come.'

The priest backs away. 'Good evening.'

'Yes,' says the Chinaman.

He should not have come but it would be an insult now not to enter the man's home. Inside, the caravan is shining: a polished floor, a mattress with a stiff, white quilt. There's the pungent smell of boiled tea, steam from a kettle. A bright light is covered by a shade. Almost everything is white, the plywood painted. There's a big indented cushion and an open book.

The Chinaman looks at the priest's feet. The dirty shoes are an insult here. The priest takes them off and leaves them outside the door, realising, as he does so, that his feet are sore. A stool is taken out. The Chinaman's hands are quick. He is a lithe man, handsome, moving freely about his home. The priest looks through a perfectly clear pane at the river and feels a fresh stab of envy.

'Yes,' says the Chinaman. 'You trouble.'

'My trouble?'

The Chinaman nods.

'I have no trouble,' the priest says.

The Chinaman laughs; he understands this is what people who are in trouble say. He takes a glass from a shelf, pinches dried leaves from a canister, pours boiling water. He fills a glass to the brim, hands it to the priest. It is almost too hot to hold. The leaves float at first then fall slowly and expand. It tastes bitter and burns his tongue.

The Chinaman stares at him. His eyes are wide open, focused. He folds his sleeves up neatly to the elbow and reaches out to touch the priest. It is three years since anyone touched him and the tenderness in the stranger's hands alarms him. Why is tenderness so much more disabling than injury? The hands are dry and warm. When they reach down from his jaw and encircle his throat, the priest swallows hard and stares at a print on the wall. The print depicts a plain, alabaster bowl and its shadow.

'Yes.' The Chinaman goes to the mattress and slaps it.

'What?' says the priest.

'Good,' says the Chinaman. 'Yes.'

The priest takes off his jacket and lies on the mattress. He lies on his back but the hands turn him over. His socks are taken off. Thumbs press his toes, his heels and move deep into the soles of his feet. The Chinaman lets out a grunt of comprehension, shifts to the priest's side and begins, with his hands, to strike him. He starts at his ankles and moves, with infinite patience, up to the back of his thigh. When he reaches his buttocks, he pushes his fists deep into the flesh. The priest feels an urge to cry out but the hands move to the other leg pushing whatever is in his legs into his torso, as though his contents could tip from one side of his body to the other. The priest slowly feels his resistance giving in; it is the old, cherished feeling of his will subsiding. Let the man strike him. It is a strange feeling but it is new. He turns his head and stares at the alabaster bowl.

Fragments of his time with Lawlor's daughter cross his mind. How lovely it was to know her intimately. She said self-knowledge lay at the far side of speech. The purpose of conversation was to find out what, to some extent, you already knew. She believed that in every conversation, an invisible bowl existed. Talk was the art of placing decent words into the bowl and taking others out. In a loving conversation, you discovered yourself in the kindest possible way, and at the end the bowl was, once again, empty. She said a man could not know himself and live alone. She believed physical knowledge lay at the far side of love-making. Her opinions sometimes galled him but he could never prove her wrong. He remembers that night in the parlour, her smooth, freckled arms. How she sat on the edge of the bed in Newry town and sewed the button back onto his shirt. The next morning, their last, they had lain in bed with the window open and he'd dreamt the wind had blown the freckles off her body. Later that morning, when she turned her head and looked at him, he said he could not leave the priesthood.

Now, the Chinaman is manipulating his hands, pulling them back from his wrists until the priest feels certain they will snap. His head is lifted, brought round in circles that get wider. Knees are placed at either side of his head. The Chinaman is dragging something from the base of his spine, from his tailbone, up through his body. There's something hard that does not want to budge but the hands don't care. Before he is ready, the priest feels something inside him folding back, the way water folds back from the shore to form another wave – and it crashes from his mouth, a terrible cry that is her name and then it's over.

After a time he cannot measure, he slowly sits up and looks about the room. He stares at the Chinaman, at his bare feet, the floor. It is hotter now and he feels hungry. The man is filling the kettle again, striking a match, as though this happens every day.

'Thank you,' the priest says at last. 'Thank you.'

The Chinaman squats beside him with a fresh glass of tea. Here is a man living happily in a clean place on his own. A man who believes in what he does and takes plea-sure in the work. The priest must give him something. He puts his hand into his pocket and feels there, Lawlor's money. The Chinaman bows when he takes it but he does not count the notes. He simply drops it into a brown jar on the kitchen table.

The priest points at the print on the wall.

'What is this?' he asks.

'Old,' the Chinaman says.

'It's empty,' the priest laughs.

The Chinaman does not understand.

'Empty,' says the priest. 'Not full.'

'Yes,' the Chinaman says. 'You trouble.'

The priest finds his socks and goes outside for his shoes. The blue night has spread itself darkly over the fields. He pushes the timber gate and listens to the sound it makes closing behind him. He stands there and looks at the world. The spring has come, dry and promising. The alder is shooting out, her pale limbs brazen. Everything seems sharper now. The night has braced itself against the fence posts. The rake is a shining thing, well loved and worn.

Where is God? he has asked, and tonight God is answering back. All around the air is sharp with the tang of wild currant bushes. A lamb climbs out of a deep sleep and walks across the blue field. Overhead, the stars have rolled into place. God is nature.

He remembers lying naked with Lawlor's daughter in a bed outside of Newry town. He remembers all those dandelions gone to seed and how he said he would always love her. He remembers these things, in full, and feels no shame. How strange it is to be alive. Soon, it will be Easter. There is work to be done, a sermon to be written for Palm Sunday. He climbs the fields back towards the road, thinking about his life tomorrow, as a priest, deciphering, as best he can, the Roman language of the trees.

Dark Horses

In the night, Brady dreams the woman back into his life again. She's in the yard with the big hunter, laughing, praising her dark horse. She reaches up, loosens the girth and takes the saddle off. The hunter shakes himself and snorts. She leads him to the trough and pumps fresh water. The handle shrieks when pressed but the hunter doesn't shy: he simply drops his head and drinks his fill. Further off, the cry of hounds moves across the fields. In his dream these hounds are Brady's own and he knows it will take a long time to gather them in and get them home.

Waking, he finds he's clothed from the waist down: black jeans and his working boots. He gropes for the clock, holds the glass close, reads the hands. It isn't late. Overhead, the light is still burning. He gets to his feet and finds the rest of his clothes. Outside, the October rain goes shuddering through the bamboo. That was planted years ago to stake her shrubs and beans but when she left he took no mind, and the garden turned wild. On McQuaid's hill, through a cloud, he makes out the figure of a man walking through fields greener than his own. McQuaid himself, herding, counting all the bullocks once again.

In the kitchen he boils the kettle, scalds the pot. The tea makes him feel human again. He stands over the toaster and warms his hands. His aunt brought up marmalade last week but there's hardly a lick in the jar. With a knife he scrapes what's left off the glass and goes out, in his jacket, to the fields. The two heifers need to be brought in and

41

dosed. He must clear the drains, fell the ash in the lower field – and there's a good day's welding in the sheds before winter comes on strong. He throws what's left of the sliced loaf on the street and starts the van. One part of him is glad the day is wet.

In Belturbet, he buys dosing fluid, welding rods, oil for the saw. There's hardly any money left. He hesitates before he rings Leyden from the phone box, knowing he'll be home.

'Come up to the house,' Leyden says. 'I'm in need of a hand.'

It is a fine house on a hill, which his wife, a school teacher, keeps immaculate. Two storeys painted white look out over the river. In the yard a pair of chestnut trees, the horse lorry, heads over every stable door. When Brady gets there, Leyden waves from the hayshed. He's a tight man, bony, with great big hands.

'Ah, Brady! The man himself!'

'There's a bad day.'

'"Tis raw,' Leyden agrees. 'Throw the halter on the mare there, would you? I've a feeling she'll give trouble.'

Brady stands at the mare's head while Leyden shoes. The big hands are skilled: the hoof is measured, pared, the toe culled for the clip. On the anvil the shoe is held, hammered to size. Steel nails are driven home, and clenched. Then the rasp comes round, the shavings falling like sawdust at their feet. All the while it's coming down, gasps of sudden rain whipping the galvanised roof. Brady feels strange pleasure standing there, sheltered, with the mare.

When Leyden rasps the last hoof, he throws the tools down and looks out at the rain.

'It's a day for the high stool.'

'It's early,' Brady says uneasily.

'If we don't soon go, it's late it will be.' Leyden laughs, his eyes searching the ground for nails.

'I've to get me finger out; there's jobs at home,' says Brady. He puts the mare back in the stable, bolts the door.

'You'll come, any road,' Leyden says. 'I'll get Sean to cash a cheque and we'll settle up.'

'It'll do another day.'

'Not a hate about it. I might not have it another day.'

As Brady follows Leyden back to town, a burning in his stomach surges. Leyden turns down the slip road past the chemist and parks behind The Arms. It looks closed but Leyden pushes the back door open. The bulb is dark over the pool table. On *Northern Sound* FM, a woman is reading out the news. Long Kearns is there with his Powers, staring into the ornamental fishing net behind the bar. Norris and McPhillips are picking horses for the next race. Big Sean stands behind the counter, buttering bread.

'Is that bread fresh or is it yesterday's?' Leyden asks.

'Mother's Pride,' Sean smiles, looking up. 'Today's bread today.'

'But if we ate it tomorrow wouldn't it still be today's?' says Norris, who has drunk up two farms. Except for the slight shake in his hand, no one would ever know.

'Put up two of your finest there, Sean,' says Leyden, 'and pay no mind to that blackguard.'

'He's been minding me for years,' says Norris. 'He'll hardly stop now.'

Sean puts the lip of a pint glass to the tap. Leyden hands him the cheque and tells him to give Brady the change. The stout is left to settle, the dark falling slowly away from the cream.

'We got the mare shod, anyhow.'

'Did she stand?'

43

'It was terror,' Leyden says. 'I'd still be at it only for this man here.'

'It's a job for a younger man,' McPhillips says. 'I did it myself when I was a garsún.'

'After three pints there's nothing you've not done,' says Norris.

'And after two there's nothing you won't do!' says Leyden, raising the bar. 'Isn't that right, Sean?'

'Leave Sean out of it,' the barman says affectionately.

Norris looks at Brady. 'Is it my imagination or have you lost weight?'

Brady shakes his head but his hand reaches for his belt. 'It's put it on I have.'

Big Sean wraps the sandwiches in clear plastic and puts them in the fridge. Brady reaches out and his hand closes on the glass. The glass feels cold in his hand. It isn't right to be drinking at this hour, and the stout is bitter.

'Have you a drop of blackcurrant there, Sean?'

'What are you doing with that poison?' Leyden asks. 'Destroying a good pint.'

Brady swallows a long draught. 'At least I didn't destroy four good hoofs,' he says, finding his voice at last.

Everybody laughs.

'Is that so?' says Leyden, smiling. 'And what would you know? There's nothing but cart horses in Monaghan.'

'Every good cart horse needs shoes,' says Brady.

'They wear down around the Cavan potholes,' says McPhillips, a Newbliss man.

'Now we have it!' Norris cries.

When the banter subsides, McPhillips goes out to place the bets. Sean turns off the radio now that the news is over. The silence is like every silence; each man is glad of it and glad, too, that it won't last.

44

As they sit there, Leyden's nostril flares.

'Which one of ye dug up Elvis?'

'Lord God!' Long Kearns cries, coming suddenly to life,'that stink would knock a blackbird off its pad.'

Leyden swallows half his pint. The shoeing has put a thirst on him so Brady, not liking to leave with the money, orders another round.

⚐

Out in the street, schoolchildren are eating chips from brown paper bags. There's the smell of fried onions, hot oil and vinegar. It is darker now and the rain is still falling. When Brady walks into the diner, the girl at the counter looks up: 'Fresh cod and chips?'

'Ay.' Brady nods. 'And tay.'

He sits at the window and looks out at the day. Black clouds are sliding over the bungalows. He thinks again of that night in Cootehill. There was a Northern band in The White Horse. They sat at a distance from the stage and talked. She had a thoroughbred yearling and a three-year-old she thought would make an honest hunter. As she talked, a green spotlight shone through her hair. They danced a little and she drank a glass of wine. Afterwards, she asked him back to the house. *If you bring the chips, I'll light the fire and put the kettle on.* They ate supper in the firelight. A yellow cloth was spread over the table. She put down wicker placemats, pepper and salt, warm plates. The cutlery flashed silver. Smell of deodorant lingered in her bedroom, a wee candle burning, and headlights were passing through the curtains. When he woke, at dawn, she was asleep, her hand on his chest. He was working then, full time, for Leyden. That morning, walking down the main street, buying milk and rashers, he felt like a man.

The girl comes with his order. Brady eats what's placed before him, pays up, and faces down the street. He has to think for a moment before he can remember where he parked the van. He passes a stand of fruit and vegetables, a bucket of tired flowers, boxes of Christmas cards, ropes of trembling red and yellow tinsel. When he is walking past the hotel, he recognises a tune he cannot name. He stops to listen, then finds himself at the counter ordering a pint. The day is no longer his own. A few more tunes are played. At some point he looks up and realises McQuaid is there, in a dark suit of clothes, with his wife. Sensing him, McQuaid looks over, nods. Soon after, a pint's sent down. On Brady's lips the stout tastes colder than the last.

'The bold man himself! Have you no home to go to?' It's Leyden. He takes one look at Brady, and changes. 'What's ailing you at all, man?'

Brady shakes his head.

Leyden looks over at McQuaid. The waitress is bringing serviettes, knives for the steak.

'Pay no mind,' he says. 'Not a hate about it. The land'll be here long after we're dead and gone. Haven't we only the lend of it?'

Brady nods and orders the drink. Leyden pulls his stool up close and waits for the pint to settle. Brady is almost sorry he came in. When the pint is ready, Leyden puts it on the beer mat, turns it round.

'Never mind the land. It's the woman that's your loss,' he says unhelpfully. 'That was the finest woman ever came around these parts.'

'Ay,' Brady says.

'There's men'd give their right arms to have a woman like that.' Leyden says, coming in tight and taking hold of his arm.

'They would, surely.'

The waitress passes with two sizzling plates.

'What happened at all?' asks Leyden.

Brady feels rooted to the stool. Back then some days were hard but not one of them was wasted. He looks away. The silence rises. He lifts his glass but he cannot swallow.

'It was over the horse,' he says finally.

'The horse?'

Leyden looks at him but Brady does not want to go on. Even the mention of the horse is too much.

'What about the horse?' Leyden persists but then he looks away to leave Brady some room.

'I came home one night and she told me I'd have to buy food, pay bills. She told me I'd have to take her out for dinner.'

'And what did you say?'

'I told her to go fuck herself!' Brady says. 'I told her I'd put her horses out on the road.'

'That's terror,' Leyden says. 'Did you have drink on you?'

Brady hesitates. 'A wee drop.'

'Sure we all say things –'

'I went out and opened the gate and put her horses out on the road,' Brady says. 'She gave me a second chance but it was never the same. Nothing was ever the same.'

'Christ,' says Leyden, pulling away. 'I didn't think you had it in you.'

❦

It is well past closing time when Brady finds the van. He gets behind the wheel and takes the back roads home. It will be all right; the sergeant knows him, he knows the sergeant. He will not be stopped. There are big, wet trees at either side of these roads, telephone poles, wires dangling. He drives on through falling leaves, keeping to his own side. When he reaches the front door, the bread is still on the step. The dog hasn't come home but he knows the birds will have it gone by morning. He looks at the kitchen table, the knife in the empty jar, and climbs the stairs.

He gets into the bed and takes his jumper off. He wants to take his boots off but he is afraid. If he takes his boots off he knows he will never get them back on in the morning. He crouches under the bedclothes and looks at the bare window. It is winter now. What is it doing out there? The wind is piping terrible notes in the garden and, somewhere, a beast is roaring. He hopes it is McQuaid's. He lies in his bed and closes his eyes, thinking only of her. He can feel his own heart, beating. Soon, she will come back and forgive him. The bridle will be back on the coat stand, the cloth on the table. In his mind there is the flash of silver. As sleep is claiming him, she is already there, her pale hand on his chest and her dark horse is back grazing his fields.

The Forester's Daughter

Deegan, the forester, is not the type of man to remember his children's birthdays, least likely that of his youngest, who bears a strong, witch-like resemblance to her mother. If occasional doubts about his daughter cross his mind he does not dwell on them for, in fairness, Deegan has little time to dwell on things. In Aghowle there are three teenagers, the milking and the mortgage.

Some of Deegan's hardship he brought upon himself. When his father passed away and left the place to his sons, Deegan, who was not yet thirty at the time, borrowed money against the place and bought them out. His brothers, who had other ambitions, were glad of the money and went off to make lives for themselves in Dublin. The night before the bank took over the deed, Deegan walked the fine, south-facing meadows. It broke his heart to mortgage the place but he could see no other way. He bought a herd of Friesians, put electric fences round the land and installed the milking parlour. Shortly afterwards, he drove to Courtown Harbour to find a wife.

He found Martha Dunne on a Sunday afternoon in the Tara Ballroom. Deegan, sitting there in a blue pinstriped suit with his beard trimmed, watched this broad-hipped woman making bold figures of eight within a stranger's arms. Her skin was smooth as a plate and her scent, when they waltzed, reminded him of the gorse when it is on fire.

While the band was playing the last tune, Deegan asked if she would meet him again.

'Ah, no,' she said.

'No?' Deegan said. 'Why not?'

'I don't think so.'

'I see,' Deegan said.

But Deegan didn't see and for this simple reason, he persisted. The following Sunday he went back to Courtown and found Martha in the hotel, eating alone. Without asking, he sat down and kept her company. While she ate, he steered the conversation from the fine weather through the headlines and wound up talking about Aghowle. As he described his home, he began to imagine her there buttering turnips, patching his trousers, hanging his shirts to dry out on a line.

Months passed and through nothing stronger than habit, they kept meeting. Deegan always took her out to supper and to dances, making sure to pay for anything that passed her lips. Sometimes, they walked down to the sea. On the strand, gulls' footprints went on for a while then disappeared. Deegan hated the feel of sand under his feet but Martha's stride was loose, her brown gaze even. She strolled along, stooping every now and then to pick up shells. Martha was the type of woman who is content in her body but slow to speak. Deegan mistook her silence for modesty and, before a year of courtship ended, he proposed.

'Would you think of marrying me?'

While the question was in mid-air, Martha hesitated. Deegan was standing with his back to the amusement arcade. With all the lights behind him she could hardly make him out; all she could see were slot machines and shelves of coins that every now and then pushed a little excess into a shoot to let somebody win. At a van a child was reaching up for candy. The crowd was getting smaller; summer was coming to an end.

Martha's instinct told her to refuse but she was thirty years of age and if she said no this question might never be asked of her again. She wasn't sure of Deegan but none of the others had ever mentioned marriage, so Martha, with her own logic, concluded that Victor Deegan must love her, and accepted. In all the years that followed, Deegan never thought but he did love her, never thought but he showed his love.

The following spring, while birds searched for the perfect bough and the crocus laboured through the grass, they married. Martha moved into the house Deegan had described at length but found Aghowle to be a warren of dim, unlived-in rooms and unsteady furniture. Dirty nylon curtains clung to the panes. The wooden floors were bare of rugs, the ceilings full of woodworm but Martha, being no housekeeper, didn't really care. She rose late, drank her tea on the doorstep and threw meals together same as she was packing a suitcase. Often Deegan came home from work expecting her to be there with a hot dinner but more often than not his house was empty. He'd stoop and find the big enamel plate with fried potatoes and a pair of eggs dried out in the oven.

Martha preferred to be out in wellingtons lifting a drill for onions or slashing the nettles along the lane. The forester brought her seedlings he'd found in the wood, sycamores and horse chestnuts which she staked about the land in places where the hedges had been broken. For company she bought two dozen Rhode Island Red pullets and a cock. She sometimes found herself standing in the barn watching her fowl pecking the seed, feeling happy until she realised she wasn't.

Before a year had passed the futility of married life struck her sore: the futility of making a bed, of drawing and pulling curtains. She felt lonelier now than she'd ever felt when she was single. And little or nothing was there around Aghowle to amuse her. Every week she cycled to the village but Parkbridge was just a post office and a public house cum shop whose keeper was inquisitive.

'Is Victor well? There's a great man, a great worker. You'll not find the grass growing under his feet.'

'You must like living up there now, do you? A fine house it is.'

'Where did he find you anyhow? Courtown? Didn't he go far enough for you?'

One Thursday, as she was about to cycle out for groceries, a stranger appeared with a trailer. A big blade of a man with a thick moustache, he parked in the centre of her yard and strode up to the door.

'Have you any interest in roses?'

There, in the trailer, the stranger had all types of plants: rosebushes, budding maples, Victoria plum trees, raspberry canes. It was the end of April. She said it was getting late for planting but the salesman said he knew that, and would not go hard on her. She asked how much he wanted for the roses, and his price seemed fair. Over tea, they talked of vegetables, how lifting the potato stalk was magic for you never really knew what it would yield. When he left, she collected hen dung with the shovel and planted the rosebushes deep in rows at either side of the hall door where she could train them to climb up around the windows.

When Deegan came home she told him what had happened.

'You spent my money on roses?'

'Your money?'

'What kind of fool did I marry at all?'

54

'Is it a fool I am?'

'What else?'

'I suppose I was fool enough to marry you.'

'Is that so?' Deegan grabbed the end of his beard as though he might tear it off. 'The hard times aren't over. It's all very well for you sitting here day in, day out. You didn't bring so much as a penny into this place. And a working man needs more than dried-out spuds for his dinner.'

'You don't look any the worst for it.'

And it was true: Deegan had put on weight, had the bloom on him that men have after they marry.

'If that's the case, it's not your doing,' Deegan said, and went out to milk the cows.

That summer her roses bloomed scarlet but long before the wind could blow their heads asunder, Martha realised she had made a mistake. All she had was a husband who hardly spoke now that he'd married her, an empty house and no income of her own. She had married a man she did not love. What had she expected? She had expected it would grow and deepen into love. And now she craved intimacy and the type of conversation that would surpass misunderstanding. She thought about finding a job but it was too late: a child was near ready for the cradle.

The children Martha bore, she reared casually, never threatening them with anything sharper than a wooden spoon. When her first-born was placed in her arms her laughter was like a pheasant rising out of the bushes. The boy, a shrill young fellow, grew tall but it soon became apparent that he had no love of farming; when the boy sat in under a cow, the milk went back up to her horns. He looked up to his uncles whom he visited every now and then in Dublin, and it was hardship to make him do a hand's turn. He would get away just as soon as he saw the opportunity.

The second child was a simpleton: a beautiful, pale boy with a pair of green eyes staring from a shell of dark brown hair. He did not attend school but lived in a world of his own and had a frightening aptitude for speaking the truth.

It was the girl who had the brains, the girl who travelled through youth same as youth was a warm stretch of water she could easily cross. She finished her homework before the school bus reached the lane, refused to eat meat and had a way with animals. While others were afraid to enter the bull's field, she could walk up and take the ring out of his nose. And she had taken a liking to her brother, the simple one. Always she was urging him on to do the things nobody else believed him capable. She'd taught him how to knot and cast the hook, how to strike a match and write his name.

Seldom did neighbours come into that house but whenever they did, Martha told stories. In fact, she was at her best with stories. On those rare nights they saw her pluck things out of the air and break them open before their eyes. They would leave remembering not the fine old house that always impressed them or the man with the worried look that owned it or the strange flock of teenagers but the woman with the dark brown hair which got looser as the night went on and her pale hands plucking unlikely stories like green plums that ripened with the telling at her hearth. After these stories they were sometimes too frightened to go back out into the night, and Deegan had to walk them as far as the road. After such nights, he always took his woman to bed to make not only her but himself sure that she was nobody's but his. Sometimes he believed that was why she told a story well.

But in that household as in any other, Mondays came. Whether the dawn was blood red or a damp, ash grey,

Deegan got up and placed his bare feet on the cold floor and dressed himself. Often his limbs felt stiff but, without complaint, he milked, ate his breakfast and went to work. He worked all day and some days were long. If, in the evenings, his eyes of their own accord were closing while he'd yet again the cows to tend, it was a solace to drive over the hill and see the lighted windows, the tusk of chimney smoke, to know his work was not for nothing. Before he retired, the bank would give back the deed and Aghowle would, at last, belong to him.

The fact that it stood in a hollow, that the walls within it were no thicker than cardboard didn't matter. Now that his parents were dead and his brothers had gone, Deegan was becoming sentimental. He remembered not how his mother had spent so much of his youth in bed with the curtains drawn or the nights when his father took down the strap saying he couldn't have it all his own way, but simpler things, plain facts. The line of oaks on Aghowle's lane were planted by his great-grandfather. No matter how hard or high his children swung, those limbs would never break. Secretly, he knew that the place gave him more satisfaction than his wife and children ever would.

Deegan is now middle-aged. If it is a stage when some believe that much of life is over, and assume that what's left is a downhill slope to be lived within the restraints of choices made, for Deegan, it is otherwise. For him, retirement will be the reward for all the risks he's ever taken. By the time his pension comes, his children will be reared. He envisages himself in Aghowle with one Shorthorn for the house. He will get up when it suits him, sort through stones and repair the orchard walls. He will take out the spade, plant more oaks on the land. He can already feel the dry stone, the oaks' blue shade. The eldest boy will marry,

have children, and carry on the name. But in the mean-
time, before he can take his early retirement and retreat
into this easy life he craves, there are children to finish
rearing, bills to pay and years of work yet to be done.

᙮

One wet day while he is working beyond Coolattin prun-
ing a line of Douglas fir, Deegan stumbles across a gun
dog. The retriever has sheltered for the night under the
trees and the forester has, in fact, roused him from a dream
of ponies chasing him through a bog. Puzzled at first by
the presence of a stranger, the retriever looks around and
then remembers yesterday. O'Donnell tried to shoot him
but then O'Donnell's rage was always sharper than his
aim. It was, quite simply, a case of the bad hunter blaming
his dog. Now this bearded stranger whose scent is all resin
and cow's milk is standing over him, offering buttered
bread. The dog eats it and lets the stranger stroke him.
    Deegan does this knowing he will some day – if no
owner comes looking – get a nice turn, for the dog is handsome. Waves of white gold run down the retriever's back.
His snout is cold, his eyes brown and ready. Come
evening, Deegan doesn't have to coax him into the car. The
dog jumps in and puts his paws up on the dash. With the
sunlight striking his coat and the wind in his ears, they
travel down hills towards Shillelagh and the open road.
    When they reach Aghowle, Deegan is glad, as usual, to
see his house with its chimney sending smoke up to the
heavens – not that he believes in heaven. Deegan is not a
religious man. He knows that beyond this world there is
nothing. God is an invention created by one man to keep
another at a safe distance from his wife and land. But

always he goes to Mass. He knows the power of a neighbour's opinion and will not have it said that he's ever missed a Sunday. It is autumn. Brown oak leaves are twisting in dry spasms around the yard. Exhausted, Deegan gives the dog to the first child he sees. It happens to be his youngest and it happens to be the girl's birthday.

And so the girl, whose father has never given her so much as a tender word, embraces the retriever and with it the possibility that Deegan loves her, after all. A wily girl who is half innocence and half intuition, she stands there in a yellow dress and thanks Deegan for her birthday present. For some reason it almost breaks the forester's heart to hear her say the words. She is human, after all.

'There now,' he says. 'Aren't you getting hardy?'

'I'm twelve,' she says. 'I can reach the top of the dresser without the stool.'

'Is that so?'

'Mammy says I'll be taller than you.'

'No doubt you will.'

Martha, throwing out barley to the hens, overhears this conversation, and knows better. Victor Deegan would never put his hand in his pocket for the child's birthday. He's picked the retriever up some place – as winnings in one of his card games or maybe it's a stray he's found along the road. But because her favourite child seems happy, she says nothing.

Martha is still young enough to remember happiness. The day the child was conceived comes back to her. It started out as a day of little promise with clouds suspended on a stiff, February sky. She remembers that morning's sun in the milking parlour, the wind throwing showers into the barn, how strange and soft the salesman's hands felt, compared to Deegan's. He had taken his time, lain back in the

59

straw and told her her eyes were the colour of wet sand.

She has often wondered since then, where the boy was, for her thoughts, that day, were fixed on the prospect of Deegan coming home. When he did come home, he sat in to his dinner and ate as always, asking was there more. Martha waited for the blood but on the ninth day after it was due she gave up and asked the neighbours in and told a story, knowing how the night would end. That part wasn't easy.

But that's all in the past. Now her daughter is sitting on the autumn ground, looking into the retriever's mouth.

'There's a black patch on his tongue, Mammy.'

That she is a strange child can't be doubted. Martha's youngest holds funerals for dead butterflies, eats the roses and collects tadpoles from the cattle tracks, sets them free to grow legs in the pond.

'Is it a boy or a girl?'

Martha turns the retriever over. 'It's a boy.'

'I'll call him Judge.'

'Don't get too fond of him.'

'What?'

'Well, what if somebody wants him back?'

'What are you talking about, Mammy?'

'I don't know,' Martha says.

She throws what's left of the barley on the ground and goes inside to strain the potatoes.

While the Deegans eat, Judge explores the yard. No doubt the place is fine. There's a milking parlour whose steel throws back his reflection, an empty henhouse with one late egg, and a barn full of hay. He walks down the lane, urinates high on the trunks of the oak trees, shits, and kicks up the fallen leaves. His urge to roll in the cow-dung is almost irresistible but this is the type of house where they might let a dog sleep inside. He stands a long time watching the smoke, considering his circumstances. O'Donnell will be out looking for him. Judge picks up a sod of turf and carries it into the house. The Deegans, who are eating in silence, watch him. He drops the sod in the basket at the hearth and, before they can say a word, goes out for more. He does not stop until the basket is full. The Deegans laugh.

'You'd have to see it to believe it,' says Deegan.

'Where did you find him anyhow?' says Martha.

Deegan looks at her and shakes his head. 'Find him? I bought him off one of the forestry lads.'

The girl gives Judge a slice of birthday cake and mashes butter into the leftover potatoes, feeds him on the doorstep.

While they are down the yard, milking, Martha comes out. The evening is fine. In the sky a few early stars are shining of their own accord. She watches the dog licking the bowl clean. This dog will break her daughter's heart, she's sure of it. Her desire to chase him off is stronger than any emotion she has felt of late. Tomorrow, while the girl is in school, she'll get rid of him. She will take him up the wood, throw stones, and tell him to get home. The retriever licks his lips and stares at Martha, grateful. He puts his paw up on her knee. Martha looks at him and fills his bowl with milk. That night, before she goes to bed, she finds an old eiderdown and makes a bed under the table so nobody can walk on his tail.

Judge lies in his new bed, rolls onto his back and stares at the drawers under the table. This is a different sort of house but Deegan will sell him just as soon as he finds the opportunity. The woman he understands: she is just the protective bitch minding her pup. The eldest fellow keeps to himself. The middle boy's scent is unlike any he has ever encountered. It is something close to ragweed, closer to plant than animal like the roots you'd bury something under. Judge, being wary in this strange place, fights sleep for as long as he is able but the kitchen's darkness and the fire's heat are unlike any comforts he has ever known and his will to stay awake soon fades. In sleep he dreams again of finding milk on the second teat. His mother was champion retriever at the Tinahely Show. She used to lick him clean, carry him through streams, proud that he was hers.

The next morning the simpleton, who sleeps odd hours, is the first to rise. Judge wakes, stretches himself and follows the boy out to the shed. They carry withered sticks in and the boy, knowing Judge expects it, does his best to light the fire. He arranges the sticks on yesterday's ashes and blows on them. He blows until the ash turns their faces grey. When the girl comes down she does not laugh at her brother; she simply kneels and, in her teacher's voice, shows him how it's done. She twists what's left of Sunday's newspaper, cocks the withered timber, and strikes a match. The boy watches and is intrigued. The strange blue flame grows bigger, changes and, at a certain point, turns into fire. Something about it makes him happy, makes him wonder. He has a capacity for wonder, sees great significance in common things others dismiss simply because they happen every day.

When Martha comes down, the door is wide open and there is no sign of the dog. She had hoped, the night before, that he would somehow run away. A cold wind is coming in. She shuts the door and walks into the scullery to fill the kettle. There on her sink is the retriever and with Deegan's good china cups, her two youngest stand rinsing the suds off his back. She doesn't really care but the girl sees her and Martha feels compelled to scold.

'Did I say you could wash that dog in here?'

'You said nothing about Judge.'

'Judge. Is that his name?'

'I called him that yesterday.'

'You'll not bathe him in that sink again. Do you hear?'

'He's my birthday present. At least Daddy bought me a dog. You bought me nothing.'

'Are you jealous?' asks the boy.

'What did you say?' asks Martha.

'Who cares?' he says. It's a phrase he's heard a neighbour use which he thinks is worth repeating.

'I care,' says the girl, reaching again for water.

Martha takes her tea out to the yard where things always seem a fraction easier. She looks down the lane. The oaks are losing their leaves so quickly now. She drinks her tea, takes the stake off the henhouse door and opens it wide. Her fowl rush past in a sweep of red feathers and dust, racing for the feed and the open air. She stoops and reaches into their nests for eggs.

She strides back in to make the breakfast, feeling treacherous. She often feels treacherous in the mornings. She wishes her husband and her children were gone for the day. Always a part of her craves the solitude that will let her mind calm down and her memory surface.

On a hot pan she watches the eggs grow white and harden. Never has she been able to eat them. This morning she longs again for sheep's liver or a kidney. She's always had a taste for such things but Deegan won't have it. What would the neighbours think? The Deegans never ate but the best and he'll not see his wife standing at the butcher's stall, ordering liver. She stands there in her apron on a Tuesday wishing she'd married another man, a Dubliner, perhaps, who would stroll down to a butcher's shop and buy whatever she craved, a man who couldn't care less what neighbours think.

With the pan spitting, she walks outside and at her loudest, shouts. The desperation in her voice travels all the way down into Aghowle's valley, and the valley sends back her words.

'My God,' says Deegan when he comes in from the milking, 'we'll be lucky if we don't have the whole parish here.'

The Deegans eat and, with full stomachs, go their separate ways. The eldest cycles off to the Vocational School. He has just the one year left and will then become apprentice to his uncle, the plasterer who lives at Harold's Cross. The simpleton heads off to the parlour, gets down on his knees and sets to work on his farm. So far he's built a boundary with dead fir cones and marked out the fields. Today he will start on his dwelling house. Before the week comes to an end, he'll have it thatched. Judge walks with the girl down the lane to the school bus. When he gets back, Martha places the frying pan on the kitchen floor and watches while he licks it clean. Without so much as a wipe she hangs it back up on its hook. Let them all get sick, she thinks. She doesn't care. Something has to happen.

She takes Judge to the wood. The sun is striking against the hazel. It is almost ten. Martha can, by now, tell what time it is without ever glancing at the clock. A blue sky is shedding rain. Some things she will never understand. Why is the winter sun whiter than July's? Why hadn't the girl's father ever written? She had waited for so long. She shakes her head at the absurd part of her that hasn't given up, and shelters for a while under the chestnut.

Judge is glad he cannot speak. He has never understood the human compulsion for conversation: people, when they speak, say useless things that seldom if ever improve their lives. Their words make them sad. Why can't they stop talking and embrace each other? The woman is crying now. He licks her hand. There are traces of grease and butter on her fingers. Underneath it all her scent is not unlike her husband's. As he licks her hand clean, Martha's desire to chase him off evaporates. That desire belonged to yesterday, has become yet another thing she may never be able to do.

Back home, she lathers her underarms and shaves them, cuts her toenails, brushes her hair and fixes it into a wet knot at the back of her skull, same as she is going somewhere. Then she finds herself on her bicycle pedaling herself all the way to Carnew in the rain. In Darcy's she buys a royal blue blouse off a rail, whose buttons look like pearls. Why she buys it she doesn't know. It will be wasted in Aghowle. She will wear it to Mass on Sunday and another farmer's wife will come up to her at the meat counter and tell her where she bought it.

When she gets back she changes into her old clothes and goes out to check her hens. Jimmy Davis had three lambs taken, and lately she feels afraid.

'Coohoooo! Cocohoooo!' she cries, rattling the bucket.

At her call they come, suspicious as always, through the fence. She counts them, goes through their names, and feels relieved. Then she is down on her knees plucking weeds out of the flowerbeds. All the flowers have by this time faded yet there is no frost in the mornings. The broom's shadow is bending onto the second flowerbed. It is almost three. Soon the children will be home, hungry, asking what there is to eat.

As she is bringing the fire back to life, Judge comes in and paws her leg. His tail is wagging. Several times he paws her before Martha realises there's something in his mouth. She kneels down and opens her hand. He drops something onto her palm. Her hand knows what it is but she has to look twice. It is an egg without so much as a crack in the shell.

Martha laughs. 'Aren't you some dog?'

Martha gives him milk from the saucepan and says the girl will soon be home. They go down the lane to meet her. She climbs down from the school bus and tells them she solved a word problem in mathematics, that long ago Christina Columbus discovered the earth was round. She says she'll let the Taoiseach marry her and then she changes her mind. She will not marry at all but become the captain of a ship. She sees herself standing on deck with a storm blowing the red lemonade out of her cup.

Back home, the simpleton is getting on well. In the parlour he has planted late, brown paper oaks to shelter his dwelling house. The boy likes being alone and doesn't mind the fact that people sometimes forget he's there.

The eldest returns from the Vocational School stinking of cigarettes. Martha tells him to brush his teeth, and puts the dinner on the table. Then she goes upstairs. She has things to think about. What she is thinking isn't new. She takes her wedding coat out of the wardrobe, opens the seam and looks at her money. She doesn't have to count it. She knows how much is there. Five hundred and seven pounds so far, she has saved, mostly housekeeping money she did not put on the table. No longer is it a question of if or why. She must now decide when, exactly, she will leave.

Deegan comes home later than usual. 'You couldn't watch that new man. He'd be gone by three if you didn't watch him.' He eats all that's placed before him, rises, and heads out for the milking. The cows are already at the field gate, roaring.

That night he goes to bed early. His legs are sore from walking the steep lines and his feet are cold but before he can turn over he is asleep. In sleep he dreams he is standing under the oaks. In the dream it isn't autumn but a fine, summer's day. A gust of wind blows up out of the valley. It is so hard and sudden – whatever way this gust is, it frightens Deegan and the oaks flinch. Leaves begin to fall. It all seems wrong but when Deegan looks down there, all around his feet are twenty-pound notes. Towards the end of the dream he is like a child trying, without much success, to catch them all. Finally he has to get a wheelbarrow. He fills it to the brim and pushes it all the way to Carnew. As he wheels it along the roads, neighbours come out and stare. The envy in their eyes is unmistakable. A few notes flutter from the barrow but it doesn't matter: he has more than enough.

When he wakes he gets up, goes to the window and looks out at the oaks. They are standing there, as always, in the dark. Deegan scratches his beard and goes over his dream. Dreaming has become the closest thing to having someone to talk to. He looks at Martha. His wife is fast asleep, the pale breast pressed against the thin cotton of her nightdress. He would like to wake her and tell her now of his dream. He would like sometimes to carry her away from this place and tell her what is on his mind and start all over again.

❧

During this mild winter, Christmas comes. The frost is brittle, the birds confused. By this time Judge's coat is immaculate, his shadow never too far from the girl's. Deegan's humour improves for he's worked overtime and caught thieves stealing Christmas trees. The Forestry Department give him a bonus cheque which he spends on new ceiling boards for the house. All through the holidays he measures and saws, hammers and paints. When he's finished with the last coat of varnish, he takes Martha to the hardware and makes her choose wallpaper for the kitchen. She picks out rolls depicting woodbine whose pattern is wasteful and hard to match.

Neighbours come to the house that Christmas and remark on how, each time they visit, the house has improved.

'Oh, an auld house is impossible to keep,' Deegan protests. 'You could spend your whole life on it and see no difference.' But he is pleased, and hands round the stout.

'Easy knowing you have a good woman behind you,' they say. 'Doesn't a woman make a place.'

'That's for sure.'

Martha is quiet. She smiles and drinks two large hot whiskeys but, despite all coaxing, refuses to tell a story.

For Christmas the girl gets an Abba record which she plays twice and commits to memory. 'Waterloo' is her favourite song. Santa slides down the chimney and leaves a second-hand bicycle for the middle child. He'd hoped for machinery for his farm – a harrow to put in the early wheat or a harvester, for his sugar beet's near ready for the factory. Sometimes he wishes for rain. Their leaves, which he made out of bicycle tyres, seem dry and are not getting any taller.

The eldest goes off to Dublin for the holidays. Deegan gives him a little money so he will not be beholden to his uncles. It doesn't matter that his eldest boy's mind is on the city. Deegan has willed him the place and knows that Aghowle will some day draw him back. To his wife he presents a sewing basket and, with egg money, Martha buys her husband a pair of Clark's plaid slippers.

On Saint Stephen's night, a fox comes into the yard. Judge can smell him, detects his stink on the draught under the door before he reaches the henhouse. Judge gets up but the door is bolted. He goes upstairs and pulls the quilt off the girl's bed. The girl gets up, takes one look at him, and wakes her mother. Martha hears the commotion in the henhouse and shakes Deegan who comes down in his pyjamas and loads the gun. The retriever's excitement grows. He hadn't known Deegan owned a gun. Together they run out to the yard. A white moon is spinning, shredding the light between the clouds. The taste on Judge's tongue is hot like mustard but they are too late: the henhouse door stands ajar and the fox is gone. He has killed two hens and taken another. Their young look demented. In the chaos they keep searching but every wing they find is not their mother's. Judge stares at Deegan but all Deegan does is fire a few shots off in the air – as though that would make any difference to a fox.

The next morning the forester goes out to pluck the hens. He looks up at the beam where he hung them but there's nothing there, just the bits of baling twine he strung them up with. Martha is already burying them in the garden. Her eyes are red.

'Such waste,' Deegan says, and shakes his head.

'We'd be hard up if we had to eat Sally and Fern. You dig them up. You eat them. I'll make the sauce.'

'You never in your married life made sauce.'

'Do you know, Victor Deegan, neither did you.'

The nights between Christmas and the New Year are long. The simpleton, with bits of ceiling boards, builds haysheds for his farm, which he crawls through. The girl writes down her resolutions and with her brother's sense of wonder reads the chapter entitled 'Reproduction' in the eldest's new biology book. Aghowle stinks of varnish and there isn't much money. Deegan is uneasy. He keeps having the same dream: every night he puts his hand in his pocket and there, his wallet, bulging with all the money he's ever earned, is cut in two. All the notes are in halves and he can convince neither shopkeeper nor bank clerk that they are genuine. Towards the end, all the neighbours stand there laughing, saying there will be no improvements now.

He dreams a strange dream also; of coming home through a blue evening feeling anxious because no smoke is rising, of walking inside and his house being empty. There is a note that makes him sad for a while but the sadness doesn't last and in the end he is a young man again on his knees, lighting the fire. After this dream he wakes and, in an attempt at intimacy, tells his wife.

Martha, still half asleep, says, 'Why would I leave you?' and turns over.

Deegan straightens himself. Such a strange thing to say. He never thought she'd leave him, never thought such a thing had crossed her mind. The house itself seems strange tonight. Martha's roses have, through the years, crawled up along the walls and, in the wind, paw the windows. On the staircase, a green shadow like water trembles. He goes downstairs feeling brittle, to get a drink. Some day it will all be over. He will get back the deed, buy a steel box and bury it under the oaks. Without Aghowle to worry about, his future will be an open hand. Martha, the mother of his children, will be happy, for there will be nights in B&Bs and brand-new clothes. They will travel to the West of Ireland. She'll eat liver and onions for her breakfast. They

70

will walk again on a warm strand and Deegan won't care about the sand under his feet.

He takes his drink in the parlour. The retriever is lying on the hearth rug, soaking up what is left of the heat. Deegan never found anyone who'd buy him. The dog is wearing a jacket of red velvet which Martha, to please the girl, has sewn during the holidays. His wife has stitched a zip along the belly and trimmed the sleeves. Deegan shakes his head. In all their time together, never once has she sewn so much as a patch onto his trousers.

He opens the ledger and looks over the bills. The price of schoolbooks is beyond reason. The thermostat in the cooler will have to be replaced. There is house insurance to renew but he can leave that for another while as he has the car to tax. He totals his income and the outgoings, sits back and sucks a breath in through his teeth. The spring will be lean but he'll be careful and get through it as he always does. One thing the neighbours can't say is that Victor Deegan is a bad provider. There isn't so much as a lazy notion in that man's head. Fifty-nine more payments. He does the arithmetic in his head. Five twelves are sixty. It will take almost five years but won't the years pass anyhow? Deegan looks again at the numbers, sighs.

The boy, who has all this time been lying inside his hayshed, looks out. 'Is it money, Daddy?'

'What?'

'Mammy says you think of nothing else.'

'Does she now?'

'Aye. And she says you can sew your *own* arse into your trousers. Why would you sew your arse into your trousers?'

'You watch your tongue,' Deegan says but he laughs all the same. The boy, like much else in life, has been a disappointment. He gets up and opens the curtains. The sky looks clear, the moon changeful. The holly this year was red with berries. He predicts a bad year and draws the curtains closed again. On the sideboard lie the girl's new copybooks, her name written neatly on their covers. Victoria Deegan. The child's name gives him pride; it is so much like his own. A cold feeling crawls up his back. He tries to think of nothing but instead he thinks of Martha saying, 'I won't leave you.'

With bills, school uniforms and a wife's unspoken desire to leave, another year begins. Martha's desire to leave wanes when a flu clouds up her head and returns just as soon as she gets well again. Judge follows the girl everywhere. When one night she runs a bath without bolting the door, the retriever gets up on his hind legs, looks over the edge of the tub and sniffs the water. It smells strange but it is warm. Before the girl knows what he's doing, he's in beside her.

In January, Dublin shops advertise their sales. Martha takes the bus to O'Connell Street but she does not go near the shops. She walks past Clery's, on down across the Liffey and winds up in a D'Olier Street cinema eating boiled sweets, crying while a tragedy concerning an Irish girl who left for America flashes across the screen. She comes back with her eldest boy and bags of rock candy, disillusioned with her thoughts of leaving. Where would she go? How would she earn money? She remembers the phrase, 'better the devil you know', and becomes humoursome. Deegan puts it down to the fact that she is going through the change of life, and says nothing. He has become more than a little afraid of his wife and, to feel some kind of tenderness, often sits his daughter on his knee.

'Tutners,' he calls her. 'My little Tutners.'

One Friday evening when he is low, feeling the pinch, Deegan drives down to the neighbour's house to play forty-five. He thinks it might cheer him up to see the neighbours and play cards but when he gets there he cannot concentrate. After five games he's lost what he normally doubles in the night, and so he gets up to leave. The neighbours do their best to make him stay but Deegan insists on going, and bids them all goodnight.

When he is getting into his car, a stranger who holds his cards close to his chest approaches.

'I understand you have a dog you'd sell.'

'A dog?' says Deegan.

'Aye,' he says, 'a gun dog. Do you still have him?'

'Well, I do.' Deegan is set back on his heel but he recovers quickly. 'I bought him last September but I've little time for hunting and it's a shame to see him wasted.'

Deegan goes on to describe a retriever. He begins to talk easily about pheasants and how his dog can rise them, how the pheasant soup tastes finer than anything you can find in a hotel. He talks about the turf basket and how it is never empty since the dog came to the house. As soon as he mentions turf, the man smiles but Deegan does not notice, for he is remembering the girl on her birthday and how she and the retriever now bathe in the same water. But it is too late to back down.

'How much would you be asking?'

'Fifty pound,' says Deegan. It is a crazy price – he will be lucky to get the half of it – but the man doesn't flinch.

'If he is what you say, I might be interested. When can I see him?'

Deegan hesitates. 'Let me think –'

'Would now suit you?'

'Now? Aye. I suppose it would.'

'Right. I'll follow you, so.'

That night Judge recognises O'Donnell before he comes through the door. He always leads with his bad foot and the foot always hesitates before crossing the door. If there is any speck of doubt in Judge's mind, it vanishes when he gets the hunter's scent. It is a mixture of silage and some kind of oil he uses to keep his hair in place. Deegan comes in first. Judge leaps up and rips his velvet jacket on the corner of the armchair.

'Well, look at you in your finery,' O'Donnell says, and begins to laugh.

Deegan, feeling slightly embarrassed, joins in the laughter. "Tis only a thing the child put on him.'

Judge does his best to escape but every door off the kitchen is closed and it is only a matter of time before the two men catch him and place him, whimpering, in the boot of O'Donnell's car.

'There now,' says Deegan. It is all he can do not to hold out his hand. 'You won't be sorry you bought him.'

'Bought him?' says O'Donnell. 'When did you ever hear of a man buying his own dog?'

As Deegan watches the tail-lights sailing down the lane he tries not to think of the girl in her yellow dress, thanking him. He tries not to think of her sitting on his lap. He tells himself it doesn't matter, that there is nothing he could have done. When he turns to go inside, something above him moves. He looks up. Martha is standing at their bedroom window in her nightdress, watching. She raises her hand and Deegan, feeling surprised, raises his. Maybe some part of her is glad the dog is gone. While he stands there watching, his wife's hand closes into a fist and her fist shakes. So, it is all out in the open.

74

Needless to say, the girl wonders why Judge doesn't wake her the next morning.

'Where's Judge?' she says when she comes down. She looks at her parents. Deegan is sitting at the head of the table forcing hard butter into a slice of white bread. Her mother is holding a cup of black tea to her lips staring at her husband through the steam.

'Ask your father,' Martha says.

'Daddy, where is he?' Her voice is breaking.

Deegan coughs. 'A man came looking for him.'

'What man?'

'His owner. His owner came looking for him.'

'What do you mean, his owner? I own him. You gave him to me.'

'In truth,' Deegan says, 'I didn't. I found him in the wood and brought him home, that was all.'

'But Judge is mine! You gave him to me.'

She runs outside and calls his name. She searches the land and all their hiding places: 'The Spaw' where he buries his bones, the tunnel in the hayshed, the grove beyond the hazels where the pheasants sleep. She searches until the knowledge that he is gone sinks in and changes her state of mind. Her father never loved her, after all. She decides she will run away but finds she isn't even able to go to school. She eats little more than a sparrow. By the time a week has passed she has stopped talking. Every evening she goes out on the bicycle calling his name:

'Judge! Judge!' is heard all around that parish. 'Judge!'

Deegan knows the girl has gone a bit mad but the girl will get over it. It is only a matter of time. Everything else in Aghowle stays much the same: the cows come down to the gate to be milked, the milk is put in creamery cans and collected. Martha's hens peck at the seed, roost for the night and lay their eggs. The pan is taken down early in the mornings, put back on its hook and taken down again. And the boys fight as always over what is and isn't theirs.

Sometimes, sitting in the wood with his flask and sandwiches, Deegan regrets what happened with the dog but most of the time it doesn't cross his mind. The consequences, not their origin, strain him most for his wife no longer speaks to him, no longer sleeps at his side.

Sometimes Martha sees herself back in that morning in the wood, throwing stones at Judge. His tail is between his legs and he is running away. He is looking back and she is feeling sorry but she knows she is doing the right thing. So much of her life has revolved around things that never happened. She grills cheese on toast but the girl won't have it. Martha sits on her bed and tries to convince her that she should get another dog, a little pup who can be the girl's own, a dog that she can love.

'We can look at the paper. There's a litter for sale outside Shillelagh. Jim Mullins has them. You'd love a –'

'What would you know about love?'

This strikes her sore. 'I do know about love,' Martha insists.

'You don't even love Daddy. All ye care about is money.'

❧

One evening when Deegan is crossing the hill, more smoke than usual is rising. Deegan sees it. Somehow he had almost suspected it. In the yard, eleven cars are parked. He recognises every one. He has never known so many neighbours to come in the one evening, nor any to come so early. Davis is here, and Redmond. And Mrs Duffy, the 'Evening Herald'. The maroon hatchback belongs to the priest.

When Deegan steps over the threshold, a massive fire is throwing waves of heat across the kitchen floor. Deegan, feeling fragile in his old clothes, bids them all good evening and takes his hat off.

'Ah, there's the man himself!'

'No man like the working man!'

'Have you enough space to get in there for your bit of dinner, Victor?'

'We're intruding on ya.'

'Not at all, sure weren't ye asked?' says Martha.

She puts a warm plate down in front of him. There's a well-done sirloin, roast potatoes, onions, mushrooms. A bowl of stewed apples is brimming with custard. Deegan sits in to his dinner, blesses himself, picks up the knife and fork. He doesn't know how to eat and be hospitable at the same time. There is no sign of the children. His wife is handing round the stout, the Powers, smiling for the neighbours.

'Drink up!' she says. 'There's plenty. Wasn't it awful about that young Morrissey chap?' Her voice is strange. Her voice is not the one she uses.

The neighbours sit there chatting, talking about the budget, the swallows and the petrol strike. They are warming up, ripe for an evening's entertainment. A little gossip begins to leak into the conversation. Redmond starts it, says he went up to the Whelan sisters for the lend of a scythe after he broke the handle on his own and caught them eating off the one plate. 'Dip to your own side, Betty!' he mimics. There is a little laughter and, in the laughter, a little menace.

The shopkeeper tells them how Dan Farrell came down and ate five choc ices, standing up. 'Five choc ices! Wouldn't he have a nice stool? And then, when he'd slathered the last, he tells me to put them on the book!'

Martha smiles. She seems genuinely amused. She reaches for a cloth, takes tarts and queen cakes out of the oven. The pastry is golden, the buns have risen.

'Would ya look at this?' Mrs Duffy says. 'They'd win prizes at the show. And there was me thinking you didn't bake.'

Martha stacks them high on Deegan's best serving plates and hands them round. She's acting, Deegan realises. She's acting well. Who would believe this didn't happen every day? The cows stand bawling at the gate to be let in but Deegan cannot move. Everything in his body tells him to get up but his curiosity is stronger than his common sense. He crosses his legs and accidentally kicks the boy who is sitting, attentive, in Judge's old bed.

'Sorry,' he says.

At the sound of his voice the neighbours turn, remembering he is there.

Davis says he walked all the way to Shillelagh but by the time he got there one of his feet got terrible sore. He took his boot off and there, inside, was a big spoon.

'Not a small spoon but a big spoon!'

'You're joking!' Sheila Roche says. It's what she always says after hearing something she doesn't believe.

Tom Kelly says he's going to do away with the milking parlour, that there is no money in milking any more. 'The farmer's days are numbered,' he says, and shakes his head. 'Sure isn't milk the same price now as it was ten year ago?'

That subject keeps them going for a while but some time

later the subject of farming dwindles and comes to a halt. A few balls of speech are kicked out into the dwindling conversation but nothing catches; they roll off into silence. The neighbours get more drink and begin to look at Martha. They turn quiet. Someone coughs. Davis crosses his legs. Because the priest is there, the request is left to him:

'I've heard you're a great woman for a story, Mrs Deegan,' he says. 'I've never had the pleasure.'

'Ah now, Father, I'm not at all,' says Martha.

'Aye. Spin us a yarn there, Martha!'

'God be good, nobody can tell them like her.'

'All she needs is a bit of coaxing.'

'Ah, I'll not.' Martha swallows what's left in her glass. Tonight, she needs a drink. Her mother always said that her father's people had tinker's blood and that this tinker's blood would take them to the road. More than once she has been mistaken for a tinker. She settles down, knowing the story she'll tell. It is only a matter of deciding where, exactly, she should start.

'Ah, you've heard them all before.'

'If you don't tell us a yarn, we'll all go home!' Breslin shouts.

'That's no way to persuade the woman,' says the priest.

Martha concentrates on the room. She has a way about her that is sometimes frightening. She looks at her feet and concentrates. Before she can begin she must find the scent; every story has its own, particular scent. She settles on the roses.

'Well, maybe I could tell ye this one.'

Deegan's wife pushes her hair back and wets her lips.

'Now we're in for it!' Davis rubs his hands.

She waits again until the room turns quiet. She has no

idea what she will say but the story is there; all she has to do is rake it up and find the words.

'There was this woman one time who got a live-in job in a guest house by the sea,' Martha says. 'She wasn't from there. She was a Bray woman who had gone down south to look for work. The house she worked in was a bright, new bungalow – much like the ones you see down in Courtown. Nothing fancy but a clean and tidy place. Mona was a big, fair-skinned woman. She was tall and pale, freckled. People sometimes mistook her for a tinker but, despite what people thought, she hadn't a drop of tinker's blood. She was a postman's only daughter and one of the things she could do well was dance. That woman could swing on a thrupenny bit and not step on the hare's ear.'

'That's a lovely type of woman,' Breslin says quietly, remembering something of his own.

'In any case, she went off this one night to a dance. It being the summertime, there was a great big crowd in the ballroom. She wasn't really looking for a man but this night the same farmer kept asking her out to dance. He was a wiry fellow with a big red beard but he was light on his feet. He led her across the floorboards same as a cat's tongue moves along a saucer of cream. They talked but the farmer could talk about nothing only the place he owned. All the acres, the trees along the lane, how fine the house was. He talked about the new milking parlour and the orchard and the big high ceilings. For the want of a better name, I'll call him Nowlan.

'Now Nowlan asked the woman if she'd meet him again and she said no but Nowlan wasn't the type of man to take no for an answer. Being the eldest boy, he was used to getting his own way. He followed the woman here, there and yon. One time she looked up from eating her bit of dinner and there he was, looking in at her through the window. He hounded the woman and the woman gave in. In the end it was easier to court him than to not court him, if you know what I mean. But he was good in his own way, would buy her cups of tea and scones, would never let her put her own hand in her pocket. And, always, they danced.

'They danced the foxtrots and the half sets and the waltzes same as they were reared on the same floor but in her heart Mona didn't really take to him. He smelled strange, like pears that are near rotten. His sweat was heavy and sweet. Really, he was past his prime. Everything was all right when they were dancing but as soon as the band stopped and he went to put his lips on hers, the woman knew the match wasn't right. But like every woman, she wanted something of her own. She thought about living in the place Nowlan had described. She could see herself out under the trees sitting on a bench in the shade, reading the newspaper of a Sunday after Mass. She could see a child there too, playing in the background, banging two lids the way children do.

'One night Nowlan asked her if she'd marry him. "Would you think of marrying me?" He said it with his back to the light so she couldn't see him properly. They were close to the sea. Mona could hear the waves hitting the strand and the children screaming. It was the end of summer. The woman didn't really want to marry him but she wasn't getting any younger and knew, if she refused, that his offer might be the last.'

'Now we're getting down to it,' says Redmond.

'Well, to make a long story short –'

'Ah, what hurry is on us?' says the priest. 'If it's long don't make it short.'

'Isn't that the very opposite of what we say about your sermons?' Davis is getting full. He has taken over the whiskey bottle, giving himself the best measures while it lasts.

The priest lifts a shoulder, lets it fall.

'My stories aren't a patch on your sermons, Father,' Martha says and looks across at Deegan. Her husband's arms are frozen across his chest. She sees the boy under the table but it's too late to back down now. She remembers the girl and the report she got from the school and carries on.

'Well, this woman, Mona, accepted his proposal. She married this man and went off to live on the farm. She thought by all his talk that the place would be a mansion so she got a terrible shock when she walked in through the door. The only thing you could say about that auld house was it wasn't damp. Nowlan had a herd of cows, all right, and a milking parlour but the furniture was riddled with woodworm and there was crows nesting in the chimneys. She made every attempt to clean the place but when she found two pairs of dentures in with the spoons, she gave up. On her wedding night she felt springs coming up like mortal sins through the mattress. And wasn't it all she could do some days not to cry.

'Nowlan spent every day and half the nights in the fields. You see, as soon as he'd won her, he paid her little or no attention. Most of the time he was gone. Where he went, Mona didn't always know. It wasn't that she thought he'd be off with other women. She'd seen him look at other women during Mass but she knew he'd never lay his hand on anyone, only herself. If he laid his hand on another woman, the neighbours would find out. It would be common knowledge and Nowlan, above all things, feared the neighbours.

'Every evening he'd come in complaining of the hunger, looking for his dinner. Mona didn't care much for food or the niceties of it but always she had a few spuds with a steak or a stew. A few years passed in that place and still there was no sign of a child. The neighbours began to wonder. They began to talk. A few comments were passed, a few dirty remarks. One man, a shopkeeper, asked her where they met and when she told him, he said, "Didn't you go far enough for a rig?" Some began to feel sorry for Nowlan. And Nowlan, knowing what people were saying, began to feel sorry for himself because – saving your presence, Father – he thought, like many a man who hasn't a babby, that his seed was falling on bad ground. Naturally, he blamed his wife for, no matter how many times they –'

'I think there must be nothing worse then being married and not being able to have a child,' says Mrs Duffy. 'I've often thought, since I had me own, that I am blessed.'

'And aren't you?' says Sheila. 'Sure haven't you the finest childer that ever walked through the chapel gates?'

'Ah, now, I wasn't saying that.'

"Tis the truth all the same.'

'Shut up, will ye?' says Davis. 'Why won't yez all shut up and let the woman tell it? I've been waiting for this one.'

'Sure wasn't I only chipping in?' says Mrs Duffy.

'Isn't that what it's all about?' says Martha.

Martha looks again at Deegan. His eyes are asking her to stop. She puts her head down and waits for the silence to rise again so she can go on. Now she is determined. She thought she'd tell it in disguise and make the disguise as thick as possible. Now she isn't sure.

'Where was I?'

'I wouldn't blame you for not knowing where you were,' says the priest.

83

'Oh, aye,' says Martha, who knows exactly where she is. 'They were married. They were married six years with no sign of a babby and then one day when Mona was on her own who comes up the front door with rosebushes only a stranger. Mona had never before laid eyes on him, didn't think he looked like anybody in that parish. Nowlan was away that day buying seed in the co-op and whenever he went to the co-op he never came back in a hurry. Mona had grown a little thinner by now. There, at the front door, stood this salesman –'

'Oh, what was he selling?' Davis whispers.

'Shut up, Davis, will ya?'

Martha pauses and lets her anger rise. They all sense it. Mrs Duffy gives her a look of sympathy but Martha isn't interested in sympathy any more.

'Roses!' she almost shouts it. 'He was selling roses. "Would you be interested in roses?" he asked her. He was a good-looking fellow, tall and cleanshaven. He didn't have that dirty beard Nowlan had and Mona was able to get a good look at his chin. She wanted to reach up and touch his chin but he was a good many years younger than herself.'

'A mere child!'

'She was robbing the cradle!'

'In the back of his van this stranger had all kinds of rose-bushes and fruit trees, everything under the sun. She bought every last one of his rosebushes and took him inside for the tea. As she was scalding the pot, he asked if she was married.

"I am but my husband is gone off to get seed."

"Has he no seed of his own?" the salesman asked. He was talking about potatoes – but then the woman looked at him.

"No," she said honestly. "He has none of his own."

'The way she said it made the salesman nervous. He got up and went over to the window. He said her hydrangea was the bluest he had ever seen. He went out and touched the bloom. It was the sun, shining on the man touching the hydrangea that attracted the woman. When she went near him, her hand touched his throat and then his thumb came up and stroked her lips. His hands were soft compared to Nowlan's.

"Your eyes are the colour of wet sand," he told her.'

Under the table the boy is concentrating on his mother's words. This is a different kind of story. This story is what really happened for he remembers the man, and the hydrangea. And then there are those things his sister taught him at Christmas, the things she read in the biology book. He wants his mother to go on, to finish it. He likes the people in the kitchen. He wishes they could be this happy all the time.

'The woman planted the rosebushes outside the hall door,' Martha continues. 'Late that night when Nowlan came home he called her a fool for spending all his good money. "What kind of a woman spends all the money on flowers?" Not only that, but he accused her of never making him a decent bit of dinner. "Spuds and cabbage is no dinner for a working man."'

'It's spoiled, he was!'

Deegan cannot stand it any more. There are some things he doesn't need to hear. She will bring in the dog, the girl. God only knows where she will stop. The neighbours are listening in a way they have never listened, as though it is the only story Martha has ever told. He stands up. As soon as he stands, the neighbours turn to look at him.

'I can't listen to them poor cows bawling any longer,' he

says. 'You'll have to excuse me.'

The neighbours push their chairs out of his way. The wooden legs screech on the floor as they let him through. When he reaches the door he doesn't know where he gets the strength to open the latch. Outside, he manages to close it behind him. He leans against the wall and does his best not to listen. In his heart he has always known the girl was not his own. She was too strange and lovely to be his.

He listens for a while to Martha's voice, trying not to hear the words. But he cannot help himself, he wants to hear the details. He strains to catch the words. Something about the way it's told tells him Martha knows he's listening. Finally, he hears his son, the simpleton, shout, 'Mammy had a boyfriend!'

Deegan's feet carry him down the yard, his hand rises to switch on lights and somehow, one by one, he gets the cows into their stalls, finds the clusters, and milks them. He is not taking his time; neither does he hurry. He is thorough, that is all. As he is finishing his work, the neighbours come out. They are leaving, coming through his front door. He had other ambitions for his front door but they don't seem to matter now. He waves to a few and they wave back but not one of them calls out.

Deegan stays for a long time in the milking parlour. He scrubs the aisles with the yard brush, rinses dung off the stalls. He puts fresh hay into the troughs, replaces a loose link on a chain. For a long time he has been meaning to do this.

Finally, he goes in. It is his house, after all. Martha hasn't gone to bed. She is still there, sitting at the fire. All around her are the vacant chairs, the empty glasses. He looks under the table but the boy is no longer there.

'Are you happy now?' he says.

'After twenty years of marriage, you're finally asking.'

'Was that all you wanted?'

Martha raises a glass of whiskey and stares at her husband.

'Happy birthday, Victor,' she says. 'Many happy returns.'

❧

A lid of silence comes down on the Deegan household. Now that so much has been said there is nothing left to say. The neighbours stay away these times. Deegan gives up going to mass; he no longer sees the point in going. He works later, eats, milks the cows and throws money on the table every Thursday.

Martha doesn't cook a breakfast any more but Deegan doesn't care. The girl goes back to school and although she gets on well, she isn't the same. There's no more talk of being the captain of a ship, of marrying the Taoiseach. The simpleton is the only one who's happy. He has turned the whole parlour into a farm. His sheds are bedded, his combine parked against the skirting board. The fields have completely taken up the floor. At the edges of his land, the nylon curtains come down like sheets of rain.

One night when he is herding his cattle, the boy hears something outside the window. It's the wind nudging the rosebushes. Or maybe it is a mouse. The boy gets up and wonders if he would be able to kill it. He has twice seen his father break a rat's back with a shovel. They are easy to kill. He stands holding the poker and goes quietly as he can towards the door and listens. He can hear the claws. When he opens the door, a dog is standing there, a stray.

Something about him suggests something else. The boy strokes him, feels the bones under the dirty coat. The dog is shivering.

'Come in to the fire,' he says, with a sweep of his hand. That's what his mother said to the stranger and the stranger followed her. Now the stray follows him, down the steps and on into his home. The boy is the man of the house now. He closes the door and tries to remember how to light a fire. It cannot be hard. Hasn't he built a whole farm by himself? He takes newspapers out of the scuttle and twists them. His sister taught him how to do this. He places the papers on the hearth of his house, where the carpet meets the plywood. It takes a long time but finally he manages to strike one of the matches.

'Damp,' he says. 'They're damp.'

The paper oaks catch fire and the boy piles high the hedges.

'It's all right,' he says to the dog. 'Come up to the fire and warm yourself.'

Intrigued, the boy watches the flames. They turn the paper black and cross into the hay barn, set fire to his roof and spread on up through the nylon sheets of rain. This is the loveliest thing he has built. He opens the door to let the draught blow it up the chimney. Some small part of the boy is upset yet he stands back, and laughs.

He looks around but the dog is gone up the stairs. When he jumps on the bed he lands on Martha.

'Judge,' the girl says. 'Judge.'

There is the smell of smoke coming up the stairs. Martha gets it too. Deegan is in the far room. He is such a heavy sleeper.

'Daddy!' the girl shouts.

Smoke is crawling through the rooms, filling up the

88

house. The boy is standing with the doors open watching the blue flames cross the ceiling boards, intrigued. Martha, in her nightdress, drags him out. Deegan doesn't want to get up. Through sleep he looks at the dog. For some reason he is glad to see him back. He turns over and tries to sleep again. An age, it seems, passes before he will admit that the house is on fire and he summons the courage to get down the stairs.

When they are all out they can do nothing more than stand staring at the house. Aghowle is in flames. Deegan breaks the parlour window to throw water on the fire but when the glass is broken, the flames leap out and lick the eaves. Deegan's legs don't work. He looks at the children. The boy is all right. The girl has her arms around the dog. There is a minute during which Deegan still believes he can save his home. The minute passes. The word insurance goes through his head. He sees himself standing out on the road but that, too, passes. Deegan, in his bare feet, goes over to his wife. There are no tears.

'Are you sorry now?' he says.

'Sorry for what?'

'Are you sorry now you strayed?'

He looks at her and it dawns on him that she isn't the slightest bit sorry. She shakes her head.

'I'm sorry you took it out on the girl,' she says. 'That's all.'

'I didn't know what I was doing.' It's the first admission he's ever made. If he starts down that road there might be no end to it. Even in his surest moments Deegan never really believed there would be an end to anything. They stand there until the heat becomes too strong and they have to back away.

They must now turn their backs on Aghowle. To some

the lane has never seemed so short. To others it is otherwise. But never has the lane been so bright: sparks and ash
are flying through the air. It looks as though the oaks, too,
could catch fire. The cows have come down to the fence to
watch, to warm themselves. They are ghastly figures and
yet they seem half comic in the firelight.

Martha holds on to her daughter's hand. She thinks of
her money, the salesman and all those obsolete red roses.
The girl has never known such happiness; Judge is back,
that's all she cares, for now. It hasn't yet occurred to her
that she's the one who taught her brother how to light a
fire. The guilt of that will surface later. Deegan is numb
and yet he feels lighter than before. The drudgery of the
past is gone and the new work has not yet started. In the
lane, the puddles are reflecting fire, shining bright as silver. Deegan grasps at thoughts: of having work, that it's
just a house, that they are alive.

It is hardest for the boy whose farm is gone. All his
work, through his own fault, is wasted. Nonetheless he is
intrigued. He looks back at his creation. It is the biggest fire
anyone has ever built. At the foot of the lane the neighbours are gathering, coming on slowly towards them.
Now they are closer, offering beds for the night.

'Who cares?' he keeps whispering as he goes along.
'Who cares?'

The Long and Painful Death

It was three o'clock in the morning when she finally crossed the bridge to Achill. There, at last, stood the village: the fisherman's co-op, the hardware and grocery, the chapel of reddish stone, every building locked and silent under the dimly burning street lamps. On she drove along a dark strip of road where, on either side, tall rhododendron hedges had gone wild and out of bloom. Not one person did she see, not one lighted window, just a few sleeping, black-legged sheep and later a fox standing fearsome and still in the headlights. The way grew steep then rounded into a wide, empty road. She could feel the ocean, the bogs; immense, open space. The turn for Dugort wasn't clearly marked but she felt confident in turning north along the uninhabited road that took her to the Böll House.

Twice on the journey she had pulled onto the hard shoulder and shut her eyes and briefly slept but now, on the island, she felt wide awake and completely alive. Even the pitch-black length of road which steeply fell to the beach seemed full of life. She sensed the high, sheltering presence of the mountain, the bare hills and, far below, where the road ended, the clear, pleasant thumps of the Atlantic on the shore.

The caretaker had told her where to find the key, and eagerly her hand searched around the gas cylinder. There were several keys on the ring but the first she chose turned the lock. Inside, the house had been renovated: the kitchen and sitting-room now combined into one long, open room.

The same whitewashed fireplace was set at one end but a new sink and cabinets were fitted at the other. In between there stood a couch, a pine table and hard, matching chairs. She let the tap run and boiled the kettle for tea, lit a small fire with turf from the basket, and made up a temporary bed on the couch. Just outside the panes, a hedge of fuchsia was trembling brilliantly in the very early morning. She undressed, lay down and reached for her book and read the opening paragraph of a Chekhov story. It was a fine paragraph but when she reached its end she felt her eyes closing, and happily she turned out the light knowing that tomorrow would be hers, to work and read and walk along the roads and to the shore.

When she woke, she felt the tail end of a dream – a feeling, like silk – disappearing; her sleep had been long and deeply satisfying. She boiled the kettle and took her belongings from the car. She had brought little: some books and clothes, a small box of groceries. There were notebooks and several scraps of paper on which half-legible notes were written. The sky was cloudy but promising, streaked with patches of blue. Down at the ocean, a ribbon of water rose into a glassy wave and fell to pieces on the strand. She felt hungry to read, and to work. She felt she could sit for days, reading and working, seeing no one. She was thinking of her work, and how exactly she would start, when the house phone rang. Several times it rang before it went silent, and then it started again. She reached out not so much to answer it as to make it stop.

'Hello?' said a man with an accent. 'This is …' and a foreign name.

'Yes?'

'The director said you are resident. I am professor of German literature.'

'Oh,' she said.

'Might I see the house? He said you might let me see.'

'Well,' she said. 'I wasn't –'

'Oh, you are working?'

'Working?' she said. 'I am working, yes.'

'Yes?' he said.

'I have just arrived,' she said.

'I have spoken to the director and he said you will let me see. I am standing outside the Böll House now.'

She turned towards the window and picked a green apple from the cardboard box.

'I am not dressed,' she said. 'And I am working.'

'It is an intrusion,' he said.

She looked into the sink; daylight was reflecting off the steel. 'Could you come another day?' she said. 'How about Saturday?'

'Saturday,' he said, 'I will be gone. I have to go away but I am standing outside the Böll House now.'

She stood there in her nightdress holding the apple in her hand and thought about this man standing outside. 'Are you about this evening?'

'Yes,' he said. 'This evening might suit you?'

'If you come at eight,' she said, 'I will be here.'

'I must come back then?'

'Yes,' she said. 'You must come back.'

When she put the phone down, she looked at it and wondered why she had picked it up and why they had given out the number. She resented, for a moment, the fact that there was a number. What had begun as a fine day was still a fine day, but had changed; now that she had fixed a time, the day in some way was obliged to proceed in the direction of the German's coming. She went to the bathroom and brushed her teeth and thought of him, standing outside. She could quickly change out of her nightdress, go out and tell him to come in and the day would, again, be hers. Instead she sat at the hearth and poked the ashes in the grate and stared at a large glass jug on the mantel. She would walk down to the shore and pick fuchsia off the hedges and fill the jug with the red, dangling blossom before he came. She would take a long bath. She looked for her watch but it took several minutes to find it, in the pocket of the jeans she'd worn yesterday. She stared for a full minute at the white face. The time, now, on this, her thirty-ninth birthday, was just past midday.

Quickly she got up and went into Böll's study, a small room with a disused fireplace and a window facing the sea. It was in this room that he had written his now famous journal, but that was fifty years ago. Böll was dead and his family had left the house as a working residence for writers. And now she was here for two weeks, working. She wiped off the desk with a damp cloth, and placed her notebooks and dictionary, her papers and her fountain pen on the surface. All she needed now was coffee. She went to the kitchen and looked through the box of groceries. She spent more time looking through the cabinets but found no coffee. She needed milk also — she would soon run out of milk – but all she wanted to do was work. This is what she was thinking when she took up her keys and drove back along the road to the village.

There, without delay, she bought coffee and milk, fire-lighters, a cake mix, a pint of cream and the newspaper. The sun was strong when she was coming back along the road, so instead of going directly home, she took the turn south along the Atlantic Drive where dwellings were few and hardly a bush was standing. She thought about how it must be to live in this place in winter: the high winds driving sand across the beaches, shearing the hedges; the relentless rain; the gulls' cold screeches – and how dramatically all of that would change once winter finally ended. On the edge of the road, a small, plump hen walked purposefully along, her head extended and her feet clambering over the stones. She was a pretty hen, her plumage edged in white, as though she'd powdered herself before she'd stepped out of the house. She hopped down onto the grassy verge and, without looking left or right, raced across the road, then stopped, re-adjusted her wings, and made a clear line for the cliff. The woman watched how the hen kept her head down when she reached the edge and how, without a moment's hesitation, she jumped over it. The woman stopped the car and walked to the spot from which the hen had flung herself. A part of her did not want to look over the cliff, but when she did she there saw the hen with several others, scratching or lying contentedly in a pit of sand on a grassy ledge not far below.

She stood there for a while watching the scene, feeling amused, then looked out over the ocean, so wide and blue under the wide, blue sky. Further ahead was a small cove where a pool of deep, clear water was edging towards the base of a white cliff. She left the car and followed a sheep track towards the cove but the path disappeared and the descent became too frightening and steep. From where she stood, she could see it all: the perfectly deep pool, the rocks and the dark tangle of seaweed under the water's surface. She clambered up the way she had come, walked to the other side of the cove, and found a different track which led to a stream of brown water, flowing off the bogs. With care she stepped over the flat brown stones, followed the slippery path and came out into the cove of white sun.

Debris had washed up from the high tide but all around

her were deep layers of glistening, bleached stones. Never had she seen such beautiful stones, clanking like delft under her feet each time she moved. She wondered how long they had lain there and what type of stone it was but what did it matter? They were here, now, as she was. She looked around and, seeing no one, took her clothes off and awkwardly stepped onto the rough, wet stones at the water's edge. The water was much warmer than she had imagined. She waded out until it deepened suddenly and she felt the slimy thrill of the seaweed against her thighs. When the water reached her ribs, she took a breath, rolled onto her back and swam far out. This, she told herself, was what she should be doing, at this moment, with her life. She looked at the horizon and found herself offering up thanks to something she did not truly believe in.

She had now reached the point where the pool broadened out to open water. Never had she been in such deep water. The longing to go out even further was strong, but she fought against it, floated for a while, then swam back to the shore and lay on the warm stones. Lying there she felt, high above, a presence on the cliff but in the sunlight she could not see properly. She lay there until her skin was dry then quickly dressed and climbed back along the steep path to the car.

Back at the house, she thought of her work while she made a dark chocolate cake. She did not make the cake from scratch but from the ready-made mix: all she had to do was dump it into a bowl and add eggs, oil and water. While she mixed the batter and poured it into a tin, a part of her mind was again preoccupied with the German's coming. She wondered, for a moment, what he would look like, how tall he would be. He might have some interesting things to say about Heinrich Böll. She felt at a loss and slightly ashamed, knowing so little about the man in whose house she was staying.

At four o'clock she walked down the road past the Protestant church towards the sea. There stood a one-roomed schoolhouse whose playground was full of dead, shaggy-headed thistles. As she stood there, a sudden breeze came over the place, and some of the thistledown came loose and floated before her eyes. On she walked to the end of the road, where a cluster of unremarkable holiday homes stood empty, their ash buckets emptied by the wind. It was colder down at the ocean so she turned back up the hill, breaking fuchsia off the hedges as she went along. Some of the slender boughs snapped easily, making a clean break, while others held on stubbornly so that she had to twist them off with her bare hands. She liked their bright red, drooping flowers, their hardy, toothed leaves. When she came back to the house, she paused to look at the sign: Please respect the privacy of artists-in-residence. She stood there for a moment looking at the words then walked into the yard and shut the gate to keep the sheep out.

Inside, she filled the big glass jug with water and arranged the fuchsia in an unruly display on the kitchen table. She made for herself a light supper of sliced tomatoes and cheese, and ate at the table with yesterday's bread and a glass of red wine. When the dishes were rinsed and put away, she lit the fire and returned to the Chekhov story.

It was the story of a woman whose fiancée was not engaged in any type of work but was known, instead, as someone who played music. She had reached the point of the story where he had taken his betrothed to the house in which they would live, and showed her all the rooms. He had a tank of water fitted in the attic, and a sink in the bed-room into which cold water ran. There was a gold-framed picture on the wall depicting a naked woman and a purple jug whose handle was broken. Something about the picture nauseated the bride-to-be; at every minute she was on the point of bursting into sobs, of throwing herself out the window and running away. Something about this story now put the woman in mind of how she had been at another point in her life, when she was falling out of love with a separated man who had said he wanted her to live with him, a man who often said the opposite of what he felt, as though the saying of it would make it true, or hide the fact that it was not.

'I love you,' he often said. 'There is nothing I would not do for you,' he often said also.

Once, when they were getting ready to go out, she had put her hair up, pinned it loosely and had chosen a long, velvet dress. She was thinner then, and in her twenties. 'I like you like this,' the man had said that night, but she'd known it wasn't true; he preferred her in a short skirt with high heels, with her hair loose, and her lips painted red.

She thought of him now as she ran her bath, with clouds of steam blowing out through the open window.

'Is there anything you would not give me?' she had once asked.

'Nothing,' he had said, instantly. 'There is nothing.'

For some reason, she had kept looking at him, and had waited.

'Well,' he had said, clearing his throat. 'Maybe the land. I wouldn't like to give you the land.'

And land, she had always known, was all he cared about.

Now she poured some rose oil into the hot water and saw again the woman in the Chekhov story and the delight the male character had felt when he saw the water running into the bedroom sink. She took up her book and found the page she had last read, and lay in the bath until she had closely read every last sentence. As it turned out, the woman did not marry her fiancée; she went instead to Petersburg, to study at the university. When she returned to her home town, the local boys cried out 'Betrothed! Betrothed!' in mockery, over the fence, but it was little attention she paid to them, and in the end she once again said good-bye to her family, and went back, in high spirits, to the city.

Now she lay back in the bath with the water growing cold and looked through the open window. Beyond the window was a blue sky, and a bare hill.

'I am thirty-nine years old,' she said, her voice sounding foolish and loud in the tiled bathroom.

At seven o'clock, she felt a strong urge to write but told herself it was not something she could do, because of the German. She would be starting, just getting warmed up when he would come and then her work would be disrupted and she would have to stop. She did not like stopping, once she had started.

Instead, she looked at herself in the mirror, and pinned her hair up loosely, and dressed. In the open room she banked the fire with turf and whipped the cream. Then she went outside with a bowl and walked around the house and picked blackberries off the briars. When the bowl was full, she looked out over the hills. The whitest clouds she had ever seen hugged tightly the brow of each, as though the hills had been on fire and the fires were now doused and smoking. She washed the berries, mashed them with sugar, and filled the cake. It looked to her a fine cake, laid there on the kitchen table. She put out white cups and saucers, small plates and spoons, two forks.

When the knock came on the door, she stood in a part of the house where she could not be seen and listened as he knocked again. She let this happen once more, then she went to the door and opened it. Outside was standing a short, middle-aged man dressed in a striped shirt and loose khaki trousers. His hair was thick and white and from his neck, on a long cord, was hanging a large decorative cross.

'Hello,' she said, giving him her hand.

'This is good of you,' he said. 'I am the intrusion.'

'Not at all,' she said. 'It's no trouble. No trouble at all.'

'You are sure?' he said.

'Of course,' she said. 'It's no trouble.'

She began quickly telling him the little she knew about the room they stood in but he wasn't ready; he held up a hand and took from his satchel a half-litre bottle of Cointreau wrapped in the white protective mesh one finds in duty-free shops.

'It is for the house,' he said.

'This is very good of you.' She took the bottle and looked at it and placed it on the table beside the cake.

'What trouble you have made,' the man said, looking at the cake.

'It's nothing,' she said, and wondered, at that moment, how he would respond if she gave him none. 'This is the old part of the house,' she began. 'The other section was built later.'

He looked briefly at the room: at the walls, the turf, the pictures on the mantel, the fuchsia. He did not seem the slightest bit interested in the room, and she wondered if he had not seen it all before. When she showed him Böll's study, he looked through the window at the falling darkness.

'So this is the famous window.'

'Yes, the sea is down there.' She pointed through the glass.

He glanced at the picture of Böll, at the framed letters on the walls. He glanced at her notebooks, her scraps of paper on the desk, and followed her along the corridor through other rooms, looking into them the way people look into rooms which are completely empty. In the last room, a long wooden bench stood under a window. She liked it here, liked the bare, working feel of it. It was the room painters sometimes used. A few glass jars stood on the bench. A folding chair was splattered with red. Standing against the far wall was a mountain bike whose back tyre was flat.

'You ride this bike?' His tone was almost accusing.

'I didn't even know it was here,' she said. 'It belongs to the house.'

At this, he leaned against the door frame and sighed. His hair, she realized, was damp, and she wondered if he hadn't been swimming. She wondered if it wasn't he who had been standing on the cliff while she was down at the cove.

'So, you are a professor of literature,' she said quickly.

'I was professor,' he said. 'I am retired now.'

'Do you miss teaching?'

'It is long ago,' he said, feeling his leather satchel. 'You are writing here? You are working?'

'Yes,' she said. 'And you? Do you write?'

'There is not much left in me to write,' he said. 'Time is running on.'

The way he said this made her wonder if he was not terminally ill. She searched his face for some sign of illness but found none. He had a healthy face and angry blue eyes.

'What do you write?' she said.

'Oh, small things, short things,' he said.

'Short stories?'

'No, no,' he said dismissively, 'longer than that but I do not have time. Everything takes too much time.'

'I see,' she said.

'Many people want to come here,' he said. 'I have seen these applications. There are many applications to come here.' He stretched out his arms and looked from one hand to the other and at all the empty space in between. 'Many, many applications.'

'I am lucky, I know,' she said, and moved back in the direction of the open room, with him following close behind.

The fire was now bright and the open room was warmer than the rest of the house. There, without invitation, the professor sat down in what she thought would be her place and turned the cup upright on its saucer. As she put more turf on the fire, she felt a strong desire to lie down and sleep.

'You'll have something to drink,' she said.

'No, no,' he said. 'I must drive.' He was looking at the flowers.

'Tea, then?'

'You are making a lot of trouble.'

'It is no trouble at all.'

She felt tired of the word, of saying it, of having him say it. She made tea, put out milk and sugar, and cut a large piece out of the cake. He smiled when she placed it before him.

'You have made this?'

'Yes,' she said. 'I have made it.'

He frowned and took a bite and then another so by the time she sat down, his piece of cake was gone. She cut another piece for him and he ate that too, and drank the tea with a great deal of milk and sugar.

'Ireland is not the same,' he said. 'People here were poor but they were content.'

'Do you think it's possible for poor people to be content?'

He lifted his shoulders and let them fall, a child's response. He could neither create conversation nor be content to have none. She thought the least he could do was chat, which, in her opinion, was where all fine conversations began. She wondered if he really was ill and if he would soon die. She thought of him lying on his death-bed and felt no sympathy.

'We were poor for long enough,' she said then.

'You are Catholic?' he said.

'I was reared Catholic.'

'But now? Do you believe?'

'Now I don't know what I believe in,' she said simply.

'I used to be like you,' he said. 'I had no faith but then I found my faith.'

She looked at him when he said this. She looked at the cross around his neck. She looked at the cake that was left and thought about how much time she had spent making it.

'Many people want to work here,' he said.

'People can work here now,' she said. 'Not long ago, we couldn't find work.'

'No,' he said, tapping the kitchen table with his finger. 'Work here,' he said, 'in this house.'

'Oh,' she said. 'Yes.'

'Many people,' he said.

A long silence grew, and hardened. She wondered what exactly he wanted. He was staring at her, waiting for a response.

'They must give it to the good-looking applicants so,' she laughed.

'Do you think so?' He frowned and looked at her face. He

examined her face closely then shook his head. 'No,' he said. 'You should have seen my wife. My wife was beautiful.'

He would have gone on, then, about his wife, would have told the entire story, had she not slowly reached for his cup and plate and put them in the sink, and let the water run over them. She rinsed the plates and cups, stacked them in the dishwasher, closed the door and turned it on, even though it was not half full. She then wiped the counter with the damp cloth and stood at the sink saying nothing more. He seemed reluctant to leave and yet he must have surely realized that she no longer wanted him there. She leaned against the counter and folded her arms and made no further attempts at conversation. She stood like this until it was almost painful to do so, and then he rose.

Slowly they walked to the door. While she was opening the latch, she had a strange notion that he might like to lock her out, so she let him out first and followed him. Outside, the night was quickly falling and the hedge of fuchsia was again trembling brilliantly in the night wind. There was something he wanted to say, she felt, as she walked him past the gate. She stood close to the gate and he stood on the road beside her. She watched him take the keys out of his satchel and waited for him to speak. They could hear the waves thumping the strand below. Three times a wave thumped the strand before he spoke.

'These people – even German people at these conference meetings,' he said. 'We do not understand each other.'

'No?'

'It is all … jargon. We do not care. We do this because we cannot write, and yet here you are, a writer, in this house of Heinrich Böll, making cakes.'

She took a breath. 'What?'

'You come to this house of Heinrich Böll and make cakes

and go swimming with no clothes on!'

'What are you saying?'

'Every year I come, and always it is the same: people going around in their night clothes in the middle of the day, riding this bicycle to the public houses!'

At this point, she heard herself; she had begun to laugh.

'You know nothing about Heinrich Böll!' he cried. 'Don't you know that Heinrich Böll won the Nobel Prize for Literature?'

'I think it is time you were gone,' she said, going back through the gate and firmly sliding the bolt across. She was standing in the yard now, watching him. He was younger than she had thought, she realized, as she saw him hopping in temper on the road, and she could no longer understand a word for his speech was now in German. For a time she stood watching the professor hopping on the public road then she walked as lightly as she could down the concrete path and went inside.

What an awful man! What an awful, unhappy man, she thought as she locked the door. Had he no sense? And to think of all the trouble she had gone to ... She looked at the cake and felt like throwing it out the window, after him. Instead, she put it in the back of the fridge and poured herself a glass of wine.

She did not really feel like drinking wine. Neither did she feel like sitting there in the house but what else was there to do? In the end she drank the wine quickly and threw more turf on the fire. She calmed down a little and opened the newspaper so as to think of something else, of other things. Our system breeds fear and loathing in separated couples, writes Jeanne Sheridan. Just this week, 80 per cent of Irish farmers said they would be in favour of legal, pre-nuptial agreements which would prevent their wives having any rights to their land. She looked at the date on the paper, turned out the lights and lay back in the light of the fire. There she took deep breaths and slowly let many things pass through her mind. She thought of the men she had known and how they had proposed marriage and how she had said yes to all of them but hadn't married one. She felt great fortune, now, in not having married any of these men and a little wonder at ever having said she would. She turned over and heard the wind stirring the hedge all around the house. All she had needed, tonight, was what every woman sometimes needs: a compliment – a bare-faced lie would have sufficed. And she had made the stupid mistake of asking for the compliment, a woman of her age. Had she learned nothing? She pondered over this for a long time and did her best to sleep but in the end she got up and boiled the kettle for coffee.

It was late when she went into Böll's study. Another day was almost gone but there she found herself, at the desk, looking out through the famous window. There was an ocean out there, a high mountain and bare hills. She looked at the scraps of paper, read over them and put them to one side. The lid of her fountain pen was stiff but she pulled it off, and opened her notebook. It was a brand new notebook with stitched, cream pages. Not until she was steadying the nib over the page did she realize her hand was shaking.

Achill Island, she wrote, and the date. She stopped then and thought of what she had done with her birthday: how she had crossed the bridge at three in the morning; of the rhododendron hedges gone wild and out of bloom. She thought of the plump hen flinging herself over the side of the cliff, and for a good reason laughed and tried to describe the hen, crossing the road. She began to describe the white stones, too, and the warm water. As she wrote, she realized the hot stones must have heated the tide, as it came in. She wrote of how it felt to lie there on the stones and the sounds they made under her feet when she walked over them. She thought of the German on the cliff, and of how it must have looked. Several times during that night, as it passed, she thought of Chekhov's light-hearted, complex heroine who never married; of the professor saying how many people wanted to come here, and how greedily he ate her cake. She thought of his temper, and began to imagine the life his wife must have had with him. At one point she looked up and saw light spilling across the land. For a moment, seeing daylight, she felt a deep longing for sleep, but she could not stop. She had just given him a name, and cancer, and was working through his illness. As she worked, the sun rose. It was a fine thing to sit there describing a sick man and to feel the sun rising. If it again, at some later point, filled her with a new longing for sleep, she fought against it, and kept on, working with her head down, concentrating on the pages. Already, she had made the incision in place and time, and infused it with a climate, and longing. There was earth and fire and water on these pages; there was a man and a woman and human loneliness. Something about the work was elemental and plain. By this time, her central character had lost his appetite and she was introducing his relatives and drafting his will. She went over the passages where his beautiful wife was offering him broth and, in doing so, realized she was hungry. When she got up, she felt stiff and pleased. She looked out at the morning striking the road beyond the trembling hedge and knew the time for sleep had come and gone. As she put the kettle on to boil and reached for the cake at the back of the fridge, she stretched herself and knew she was preparing for his long and painful death.

Surrender
(after McGahern)

For five days the sergeant kept the letter in the inside pocket of his uniform. There was something hard in the letter but his desire to open it was matched by his fear of what it might contain. Her letters, in recent times, without ever changing course, had taken on a different tone and he had heard that another man, a schoolteacher, was grazing a pony on her father's land. Her father's fields were on the mountain. What grazing would be there was poor and daubed with rushes. If the sergeant was to do as he had intended, there was but little time. Life, he felt, was pushing him into a corner.

All that day, he went about his duties. If Doherty, the guard in the dayroom, found him short, he did not pass any remarks, for the length of the sergeant's fuse was never disputed. It was a wet December day and there was nothing to be done. Doherty kept his head down and went over the minute particulars of the permit once again. Turning a page, he felt the paper cold against his skin. He looked up and stared, with a degree of longing, at the hearth. The fire was so low it was almost out. The sergeant insisted always on a fire but never a fire that would throw out any decent heat. The guard rose from the desk and went slowly out into the rain.

The sergeant watched him as he came back and positioned two lumps of timber at either side of the flame.

'Is it cold you are?' said the sergeant, smiling.

'No more than usual,' answered Doherty.

'Pull up tight to her there, why don't you?'

'It's December,' said the guard, reasonably.

'It's December,' mimicked the Sergeant. 'Don't you know there's a war on?'

'What does that have to do with anything?'

'The people of this country love sitting in at the fire. At the rate we're going, we may go back to Westminster to warm our hands.'

Doherty sighed. 'Should I go out and see what's happening on the roads?'

'You'll go nowhere.'

The sergeant stood up and put his cap on. It was a new cap, stiff, with a shining peak. When he reached out for the big black cape at the back of the door, he threw it dramatically over his shoulders. Never once had the guard seen him rush. Every move he made was deliberate and enhanced by his good looks. It was hard not to look at him but he was not, in any case, the type of man you'd turn your back on. If his moods often changed, the expression in his eyes was always the same, intemperate blue. The men who had fought with him said they couldn't ever predict his moves. They said also that his own were always the last to know. He had taken risks but had shown a strange gift for reading the enemy.

The timber spluttered into flame and its light momentarily struck the steel buttons of the sergeant's tunic. He bent over, folded the trouser legs and secured the bicycle clips. When he opened the door, the wind blew a hard, dappled rain over the flagstones. The sergeant went out and stood for a moment, looking at the day. Always, he liked to stand for a moment. When he turned back to Doherty, the guard felt sure he could read his mind.

'Don't scorch the tail of your skirt,' he said, and went off without bothering to close the door.

Doherty got up and watched him cycling down the barracks road. There was something half comical about the sergeant and his bike going off down the road but the remark lingered.

It was the easiest thing in the world to humiliate somebody. He had said this aloud at his wife's side in bed one night, in the darkness, thinking she was asleep, but she had answered back, saying it was sometimes harder not to humiliate someone, that it was a weakness people had a Christian duty to resist. He had stayed awake pondering the statement long after her breathing changed. What did it mean? Women's minds were made of glass: so clear and yet their thoughts broke easily, yielding to other glassy thoughts that were even harder. It was enough to attract a man and frighten him all at once.

The barracks was quiet but there was no peace; never was there any peace in this place. Winter was here, with the rain belting down and the wind scratching the bare hills. Doherty felt the child's urge to go out for more timber, to build up the fire and make it blaze but at any moment the sergeant could come back and as little as that could mean the end. His post was nothing more than a fiction and could easily be dissolved. All it would take was the stroke of a pen. He pulled the chair up to the fire and thought of his wife and child. Another was on the way. He thought about his life and little else until he realised his thoughts were unlikely to reach any conclusion; then he looked at his hands, stretched out to the flame. What the sergeant wouldn't say if he came back and saw the firelight on his palms.

Down the road, the sergeant had dismounted and was standing still under the yews. The yews were planted in different times, and it gave him pleasure to stand and take their shelter. The same dark smoke was still battering down on the barracks roof. He'd stood there for close to an hour, on watch, but the quality of the smoke hadn't changed; neither was there any sign of Doherty going back out to the shed. *The way you rear your little pup, you'll have your little dog.* As soon as the rain eased, he moved out from the patch of sheltered ground and pushed on for town.

Further along the road, a couple had stopped and was talking. The youth, a MacManus off the hill, was leaning over the saddle of his bike with his cap pushed well back off his face. The girl was laughing but as soon as she laid eyes on the sergeant, she went still.

'A fine day it is for doing nothing,' said the sergeant expansively. 'Wouldn't I love to be out in the broad daylight sweet-talking girls?'

The girl blushed and turned her head away.

'I better be going on, Francie,' she said.

The youth held his ground.

'Don't you know it's the wrong side of the road you're on?' demanded the sergeant. 'Does the youth of this country not even know which end of ye is up?'

The young man turned his bicycle in the opposite direction.

'Does this suit you any better?' He was saying it for the girl's benefit but the girl had gone on.

'What would suit me is to see the youth of this country rolling up their sleeves,' the sergeant said. 'Men didn't risk their lives so the likes of ye could stand around idle.'

If we can't be idle, what can we be? the young man wanted to say but his courage had gone, with the girl. He threw his leg over the crossbar and rode on, calling after her. The girl did not look back and kept her head down when the sergeant passed. The sergeant knew her mother, a widow who gave him butter and rhubarb in the summertime but all she had was a rough acre behind the house. As it turned out, there was hardly a woman in the entire district with land.

He rode on into the town and leant his bicycle against Duignan's wall. The back door was on the latch. He pushed it open and entered a smoky kitchen whose walls were painted brown. Nobody was within but there was the smell of bread baking and someone had recently fried onions. A pang of hunger struck him; he'd gone without since morning. He went to the hearth and stared at the cast-iron pan on its heavy iron hook, the lid covered in embers. Close by, a cat was washing herself with a dirty paw. Talk was filtering in from the front room that served as a shop. The sergeant could hear every word.

'But isn't he some man to cock his hat?'

'What do they see in him at all?'

'It's not as though he hasn't the looks,' said another.

'Sure hasn't he the uniform?'

'A cold bloody thing it would be to lie up against in the middle of the night,' and there was a cackle that was a woman's laughter.

The sergeant grew still. It was the old, still feeling of having the upper hand – a feeling that made lesser men freeze – but the sergeant came alive. He felt himself back under the gorse with a Tommy in the sight of his gun; the old thrill of conspiracy, the raw nerve. He was about to stand closer to the shop door when suddenly it opened and the woman came in. She hardly paused when she saw him.

'Hello, Sergeant!' she called out, same as he was far away.

The banter in the shop drew to a sharp halt. There was a

rough whisper and the clink of porter bottles. The woman came towards the pan with a cloth and swung the hook away from the fire. She removed the iron lid without letting an ember fall and took up the loaf. It was a white loaf with a cross cut deep into the surface of the dough. The sergeant had not seen a white loaf in months. Three times the woman rapped it with her knuckles and the sound it made was a hollow sound.

The sergeant had to hand it to her: her head was cool. There were few women in the country like her left. She went to the shop door and without looking beyond, shut it.

'I don't suppose those pigeons came in to roost?'

'They came in last night,' she said.

'They didn't all come?'

'They're all there. The even dozen, fresh from the barrow.'

'A fine price they must be.'

When she told him what price they were, a fresh thrill ran down the entire length of his body. It was almost twice what he had anticipated and the extravagance was, in his experience, without comparison but he hid his pleasure.

'I suppose I'll have to take them now,' he grunted.

'It's as you please,' the woman said.

The shop door flew open and a small boy, one of her troops, ran in from the shop.

'Slide the bolt there, Sean, good boy,' the woman said.

The boy leant against the door until the latch caught then slid the bolt across. He drew up close to the woman and stared at the loaf.

'Is there bread?' the boy asked, tilting his head back. The boy's face was pale and there were dark circles under his eyes.

'You can have it when it cools,' said the woman, propping the loaf against the window. She threw the bolt on the back

door and opened the lower part of the dresser. The light,
wooden crate was covered by a cloth. When she pulled the
cloth away, the sergeant got their scent. They lay on a bed of
wood chippings, each wrapped in fine, pink tissue.

The boy leaned in over the table and stared.

'What are they, Mammy?'

'They're onions,' she said.

'They're not!' he cried.

'They are,' she said.

The boy reached out to stroke the tissue and stared up at
the sergeant. The sergeant felt the boy's hungry gaze. He
took the tissue off each one and lifted it to his nose before
he pushed back his cape and reached into his pocket for
the money. As he was reaching in, his fingers lingered
unnecessarily over the envelope and he realised his hand
was half covetous of the letter. The woman wrapped the
crate in a flour sack while the sergeant stood waiting.

'Is it for Christmas you be wanting them, Sergeant?'

'Christmas,' he said. 'Ay.'

She counted out the money on the kitchen table, and
when he offered her something extra for the loaf, she
looked at the boy. The boy's face was paler now. His skin
was chalky. When he saw his mother wrapping the loaf in
the brown paper, he began to cry.

'Mammy,' he wailed. 'My bread!'

'Hush, a leanbh. I'll make you another,' she said. 'I'll do
it just as soon as the sergeant leaves.'

The sergeant took the parcel out the back and tied it care-
fully on to the carrier of his bike. He was ready now for the
barracks but he walked back through the kitchen, unlocked
the door and entered the shop. The talk that had seized up
when his presence was made known had risen back to neu-
tral speech. This, too, seized up on his entry. Walking in

through the silence, he felt the same old distance and superiority he always felt. He was reared near here, they knew his people but he would never be one of them. He stood at the counter and looked at the stains on the dark wood.

'Isn't it a harsh day?'

Always, there was someone who could not stand the silence. This was the type of man who, in other circumstances, could get another killed.

'It's a day for the fire,' said another.

The sergeant hoped one of them would open his gob and make an open strike but not one of them had the courage. To his face, their talk would stay in the shallow, furtive waters of idle banter; anything of significance they had to say would be said just after he was gone. He paused at the front door where a calendar was hanging from a nail. He studied it closely though he well knew the date. Standing there, looking at the month of December, a blade of conviction passed through him. He opened the front door and went out into the rain without having uttered a word.

'Well!' said Duignan, watching the sergeant pushing his bike eagerly up the road.

'Whoever would have thought it?'

'If you want to know me, come live with me!'

The porter bottles came back out. Duignan took a draught, straightened himself and put his hands behind his back. In a perfect imitation, he slowly marched over to the wall and put his nose against the calendar.

'It isn't December?'

'Ay, Sergeant.'

'Do you think oranges would be ripe at this time of the year?'

As soon as he mentioned the word, there was a ripple of laughter. Each man, in his own mind, had a vision of the sergeant, the big IRA man, sitting into the feed of oranges. Duignan went to the counter and sniffed the wood. Stiffly, he swung back towards the men.

'It isn't porter I smell?'

'It's on the stage you should be!'

'No, Sergeant!' cried another. "Tis oranges!'

Duignan carried on. There were fresh waves of laughter but it did not come to a head until the woman, her hands covered in flour, came in from the kitchen asking what, in the name of God, it was that had them so entertained?

The sergeant saw all this in his mind as he pushed his bicycle back to the barracks in the rain. Let them laugh. The last laugh would be his. The rain was coming down, hopping off the handlebars, his cape, the mudguard. It was down for the evening. There had not been a dry day for over a week and the roads were rough and sloppy.

When he reached the dayroom, he softly pushed the door open and there was Doherty, fast asleep, in the chair. The sergeant stole over to the desk, lifted the box of papers, and let it fall. Doherty woke in a splash of fear.

'I think it's nearly time that you were gone out of this!' the sergeant cried.

'I didn't –'

'You didn't! You didn't what?'

'I didn't –'

'You didn't! You didn't! Get up off your arse and go home!' the sergeant cried. He looked at the ledger. 'Did you not even bother your arse to record the rain?'

The guard stumbled out, half asleep, into the rain and read the gauge. All this was new to him. He came back and wrote a figure in the book and signed it.

'I hope you'll be in better form tomorrow,' Doherty said, blotting the page.

'I'll be as I am,' said the sergeant. 'And don't think just because you're getting off early that you'll not have to make up for it some other day.'

'Amn't I always here,' sighed Doherty.

'Do you think I haven't noticed? Amn't I tripping over you?'

'I do whatever –'

'But are you ever useful? That's the question. If you're of no use, then mightn't you be as well off elsewhere?'

Doherty looked at him and put his coat on. 'Is there anything more?'

'That'll be all,' the sergeant clipped. 'It's clearly as much if not more than you're able for. God help us, but I can't help but think sometimes that the force mightn't be better off with a clatter of women.'

The guard put on his coat, went out, and softly closed the door. The sergeant went to the window and watched him, how eagerly he pedalled on home. Doherty could ill afford to lose his post, the sergeant knew. He watched him until he had turned the corner then he went out for the coal.

The coal was a turn from a Protestant for whom he'd done a favour. He pushed the poker deep into the fire and raked over all the old timber. He placed lumps of coal on the embers knowing, before long, that it would blaze. He wheeled the bike up close to the hearth and untied the parcel. Then he took off the clips and hung his cape on the back of the door and sat down. There was relief in sitting down, in being alone, finally.

He looked at the marks of the tyres, of his feet, of the rain dripping off his cape onto the flagstones. He looked at these marks that he had made until the fire had warmed the room and the floor was dry. Then he took his tunic off and opened the letter. As soon as he opened the letter, the ring fell into his hand but his hand was expecting this. He looked at it briefly and went on to read:

December 9th

Dear Michael,

I have decided it is impossible for us to go on. I have waited long enough and this ring, which I took as a token of your affection, is now an ornament. Nothing is as I had expected. I had thought that we would be married by now and getting on with our lives. I don't know what it is you are doing up there or why you stay away. It must not be convenient for you to continue on with this engagement and it no longer suits me.

The time has come for us to be together or remain apart. I see no cause for any further delay. I hear you are throwing your hat at other women. You were seen outside McGuire's last week and the week before. If your heart has changed, it is your duty to let me know. I enclose your ring and pray God this finds you in good health as we are all down here.

Yours,

Susan

It was as he suspected: she was calling him in. He felt solace in the knowledge that he was right and yet it struck him sore that he had hoped it might be otherwise. Hope always was the last thing to die; he had learned this as a child and seen it, first hand, as a soldier. He held the ring up to the fire and looked at it. The stone was smaller than he had realised and the thin gold band was battered as though she hadn't bothered to take it off while labouring. He did not read over the letter again; the message was clear. He folded it back as it was, placed it in the heavy metal box and locked it. He placed the key and the ring on the desk and rolled up his sleeves.

The room was warm and the chain, at this stage, would be dry. The firelight was striking the rims, the handlebars, the spokes. He turned the bicycle upside-down and, with one hand slowly turning the pedal, he placed the nozzle of the oil-can against the chain. Oiling it, watching the chain going round, it struck him how perfectly the links engaged the sprocket, how the cogs were made for the chain. Somewhere, a man believed he could propel himself using his own weight. He had seen it in his mind and went on to make it happen. Oiling the bike stoked up the old pleasure he had felt in cleaning the guns: forcing the cloth down the length of the barrel, dull gleam of the metal, how snugly the bullet slid into the chamber. Everything was made for something else in whose presence things ran smoothly.

He had once, as a child, knocked the sugar bowl off the table. The sugar had spilled and was wasted, for it could not be sieved out from the glass. He could see it still, the bright shock of it on the flagstones. His mother had taken him out to the bicycle and spun the wheel, holding his fingers at an angle, tight to the spokes. It went on for an age and the pain he felt could not have been worse had she actually dismembered him. It was one of the first lessons he had learned and he would carry it all through life.

Now, he felt a childish pride in owning the bike. He turned it right side up and pumped the tyres until he felt hot and satisfied. When he was sure the tyres could take his weight for the distance, he propped the bike against the desk. Then he took the crate from the sack and positioned himself at the hearth.

In reaching out, he hesitated but the fruit he chose felt heavy. The rind did not come away easily and his thumbnail left an oily track over the flesh. When he tasted it, it tasted sweet and bitter all at once. There were a great many seeds. He took each seed from his mouth and threw it on the fire. Juice was staining his uniform but he would leave a note for Doherty to take it down to the Duignan woman and have it pressed. Before he had swallowed the last segment of the first orange his hand was reaching out for the next. This time he kept his thumbnail tight to the skin so as not to break to the flesh. The peelings singed for while on the open coals but shrank and in time became part of the fire.

His knowledge of women swept across his mind. He tried to think of each one separately – of what she said or how, exactly, she was dressed – but they were not so much mixed up in his mind as all the one: the same bulge at the top of the stocking, the shallow gasp, the smell of malt vinegar in their hair. How quickly all of that was over. He ate the oranges and thought about these women, concluding that there was little difference between them. By the time the last seed was on the coals, he was glutted.

'Another casualty,' he said aloud in the empty room.

The clock on the wall ticked on and the rain was beating strong and hard against the barracks door. He burned the crate and threw the coal dust on the embers. When he was sure no evidence of how he had spent the night remained, he lit the candle and climbed the stairs, feeling a shake in himself that made the light tremble. He did not take off his clothes. He got into the bed as he was and reached out for the clock. As he wound it and felt the spring tighten, the old desire to wind it until it seized came over him but he fought against it, as always, and blew the candle out. Then he rolled over into the middle of the cold bed. When he closed his eyes, the same old anxiety was there shining like dark water at the back of his mind but he soon fell asleep.

Before first light, he groped his way blindly to the outhouse and felt the oranges passing through his body. There was a satisfaction in this that renewed and deepened the extravagance, all at once. When he came inside, he lit the lamp, made tea and buttered some of the white bread. He took the razor off the shelf, sharpened it on the leather strap, and shaved. There were unaccountable shadows in the mirror but they did not distract him. He washed, changed into his good brown suit, gathered up the ring and key and went outside to look at the day. No rain was falling but there were clouds stacked up on one side of the sky.

He wrote the note for Doherty, put on the clips and threw the cape over his shoulders. When he got up on the saddle, he felt the springs give under his weight. He reassured himself that he had the ring, the key, and stood on the pedals, to get started. Soon he was labouring over the hills, knowing full well that the days of idling and making women blush were coming to a close. A cold feeling surged through him. It was new to him and like all new feelings it made him anxious, but he rode on, composing the speech. By the time he was pushing on for her part of the country, he grew conscious of the rain and the noise it made, the rattle of it like beads on the handlebars.

When he entered her townsland he saw the rushes and knew the clay beneath them was shallow clay. With a bitter taste in his mouth, he faced up the mountain but before he was halfway up, his breath gave out and he had to dismount. Marching on, he could feel his future: the woman's bony hand striking a hollow sound in the loaf and the boy with the hungry gaze asking for bread.

Night of the Quicken Trees

In every house in the country long ago the people of the house would wash their feet, the same as they do now, and when you had your feet washed you should always throw out the water, because dirty water should never be kept inside the house during the night. The old people always said that a bad thing might come into the house if the feet water was kept inside and not thrown out, and they always said, too, that when you were throwing the water out you should say 'Seachain!' for fear that any poor soul or spirit might be in the way. But that is neither here nor there, and I must be getting on with my story . . .

From 'Feet Water', an Irish fairy tale

Shortly after the priest died, a woman moved into his house on the Hill of Dunagore. She was a bold spear of a woman who clearly wasn't used to living on the coast: not five minutes after she'd hung the wash out on the line, her clothes were blown halfway up the bog. Margaret Flusk had neither hat nor rubber boots nor a man. Her brown hair was long, flowing in loose strands like seaweed down her back. She wore a big sheepskin coat that fitted her to perfection and when she looked out at the mortal world it was with the severity of a woman who has endured much and survived. When she moved to Dunagore she was not yet forty but it was past the time when she could bear a child. That power had left her years ago and always she blamed it on that night of the quicken trees.

The priest's house stood on the highest point of the hill beside the mast whose evening shadow fell into her rooms. It was joined to another cottage of equal size and they both looked down like two still hares across the Cliffs of Moher. It was autumn when she came. The swallows were long gone and any blackberry still clinging to its briar had begun to rot. The house smelled of the priest. Margaret dragged anything she didn't want down to the bottom of the haggard and set fire to it. Being superstitious, she kept his clothes. If she gave his clothes away he'd not have to go naked in the next world. She painted all the walls and ceilings with a bucket of white emulsion, disinfected the floors, the doorstep and rubbed the window panes until they squealed under the cloth, for, although she did not come from Clare, she knew nothing good ever happens in a dirty house.

When she got the chimney swept, she tore across the fields towards a farmhouse where smoke was rising. Soon after, she was running back with a shovel full of embers, her long legs stretching uneasily over the bog. After that, smoke was always rising. Neither was she gone nor did she sleep long enough to let the fire die. In fact, she liked getting up while the stars were still in the sky. It gave her satisfaction to see a star falling. If she believed in the forces of nature, she was yet determined to avoid bad luck. She'd had her share of bad luck so now she never threw out ashes of a Monday or passed a labourer without blessing his work. She shook salt on the hearth, hung a Saint Bridget's cross on the bedroom wall and kept track of changes in the moon.

When she got the house clean, she drove down the hill and around the coast to Ennistymon. These roads were narrow and steep. She could hear bog water rushing through the ditches. Beyond stone walls, bony cattle and small flocks of long-woolled sheep grazed the sod. Ponies stood with their backsides to the wind as though the wind would fertilise them. Every creature seemed capable or on the verge of flight.

Once, when Margaret was a child, her mother had gone on a pilgrimage to Knock and came back with sticks of candy. Margaret waited for a windy day, opened the umbrella and jumped off the boiler-house wall, believing she would fly, and landed with a broken ankle on the car-road. If only, in her adult life, her unfounded beliefs could be so abruptly disproved. To be an adult was, for the greatest part, to be in darkness.

Down in the village a crazy, white-haired man was standing on the bridge, directing traffic:

'Quick! Quick! Winter is round the corner!'

She bought flour and sugar, oatmeal, buttermilk and tea, peas and beans, spuds and salt fish, brought it home and baked a loaf. When it got dark at five o'clock, she went outside and lifted her skirt and squatted in the grass. She wanted to pass water on every blade of grass around her house, she could not say why. The grass was long and sour up there. Dunagore was a strange place without so much as a tree, not a withered leaf to be seen in autumn, just the shivering bogland and all the gulls wheeling around, screeching under restless clouds. The landscape looked metal, all sturdy and everlasting but to Margaret, coming from a place of oak and ash, it was without substance. There would be no shade in summer, no fields of barley turning yellow in the month of August. The skies in the east would now be obscured by falling leaves, their heifers would be in the barn, dairy cows chained to the stalls.

The next morning when Margaret went out to empty the ash bucket, the wind blew it back into her eyes, blinding her. When she came inside she decided she would stay in that house for as long as she could without harming anybody or letting anybody harm her. If either one of these things happened, she would move on. She would keep her course, get in a boat and cross over to the Aran Islands, go as far west as she could without leaving Ireland. But until then, she would do her best to keep people at arm's length for people were nothing but a nuisance.

Not every man can sharpen a scythe or cut turf. Stack, the forty-nine-year-old bachelor who lived next door, had a bald head and seeds of grey in his eyes. He'd lived and worked the land with his father all his life until his father

133

died. He was thirty-eight when his father passed away and now he was left with all the bogs and an income from the turf. He did not live alone but with Josephine, the sleek brown goat who had the run of the house. By day she stared into the fire and at night she took up more than half of the bed. Stack milked her every day, rubbed Palmolive on her teats and always remembered to bring her fig rolls from the town. He had courted a small farmer's daughter outside Lehinch for twelve years, bought her six hundred and twenty-four Sunday dinners but she wouldn't even let him touch the hem of her skirt or push the hair back out of her eyes so he could see her properly. Once she got a bit drunk and he placed his hand on her bare knee as they sat in the car outside her back door but that was all. In the end, she went off and married a man who sold stone and Stack found Josephine through an advertisement in the *Farmer's Journal*.

Stack couldn't bear to part with anything. The spare room was packed to the ceiling with his father's fishing rods, his mother's sewing machine, weed killers, jam jars, the old solid-fuel cooker. He kept all the clothes he'd ever worn, from his matinée coats to the trousers he'd recently grown out of, and kept the door closed because Josephine liked to go in there and eat his mother's slippers.

Stack did not like to think he would ever become like the new generation. Young people couldn't catch a fish or skim cream off milk. They went around in cars they couldn't afford, with small children who'd never tasted their mother's milk, committing adultery at the drop of a hat. In fact, hats didn't drop fast enough for them. They drank beer straight from the bottle, came back from America and Prague looking for pizzas, and couldn't tell a common potato from a Victoria plum. And now a woman was living next door, setting fire to the priest's good furniture, walking the roads with her hair all tangled same as she didn't own a comb.

Time passed and little happened in Dunagore. Wind off the Atlantic pushed the clouds one way and then the other, blew eerie notes through the mast, blew gates open. Cattle and sheep escaped, went roving and were captured. The postman hardly ever stopped at Margaret's except to deliver a bill for the electricity. Once, a middle-aged man came up to her door and asked her to sign a petition to get the potholes filled on the road. While she signed her name his eyes crawled over her frame.

'Would you be any relation to the priest?' he asked.

'Why, do I look like him?'

He looked up at her nostrils, the gypsy eyes and the waiting mouth.

'You don't look like anybody,' he said, and went next door to get the turfman's signature.

Margaret slept well, ate plain food and kept walking to the edge of the sea and back. Sometimes, she walked all the way to Moher and looked down over the cliffs and frightened herself. Sometimes, when she was down there with the rain drenching her hair and her sheepskin, she thought of the priest.

The priest was her first cousin. He used to come to their house every summer to make the hay. He would come with the fine weather, sit on top of the hayrick at her side, dig new potatoes, sharpen his appetite, pull scallions and eat them raw. Margaret was a teenager. Skies were blue back then. As a young man, he said they would marry, that they would get the bishop's permission, rear Shorthorns and have two children, a pigeon's clutch. Margaret could see him coming in from the fields with a handful of clover, saying the meadow was without comparison. And then he went off to the seminary, became the pride of a family who no longer called him by his name:

'Another drop of gravy, Father?'

'Do you think there's such a place as Limbo, Father?'

'Did my father say where he was going, Father?'

Even though he came back every summer to make the hay, he never again sat on the ditches combing knots out of her hair, talking about the children they would have. Summers passed and the whole family, instead of putting on the record player and opening the stout when the hay was safe on the loft, would kneel and answer his rosary.

Margaret tried not to think of the priest. After her walks, she sat with her feet in a basin of soapy water listening to Raidió na Gaeltachta, or got into his bed with the hot-water bottle, trapping lamplight in the right angle of his books. Sometimes she came across a passage he'd under-lined but the words held no great meaning. Nothing in the house she'd come across meant anything. Sometimes she saw his shadow at the bedside, felt his cold presence shad-owing hers and saw again his open collar, the hayseed trapped in his cuffs, but that was only his ghost.

If she wondered, before she slept, what her neighbour was doing in his bed at the far side of the wall, she didn't dwell on it. She tried not to dwell on anything. Putting the past into words seemed idle when the past had already happened. The past was treacherous, moving slowly along. It would catch up in its own time. And in any case, what could be done? Remorse altered nothing and grief just brought it back.

No doubt she was the subject of curiosity. Some said her people were all dead and that the priest was her uncle, that he'd taken pity on her and left her the house. Others swore she was a wealthy woman whose husband had run off with a teenager and that her heart was broken. Down in the pub when it got late, it was common knowledge that the priest had been in love with her, that she'd had his child and lost it, that he hadn't gone off to the mission at all that time he'd gone off to the mission.

On All Soul's night, the middle-aged man who'd given her the embers banged on her door, but Margaret just stood there staring him down through the glass. Eventually, he went away. And women said she must be going through the change of life:

'The new moon takes a terrible toll on women like her,' one woman down in Lisdoonvarna said, feeling the wilted heart of a cabbage.

'Oh, it would,' said another. 'The moon'll pull at her like the tide.'

Stack, like every man who has never known a woman, believed he knew a great deal about women. He thought about Margaret Flusk as he drove home from Lisdoonvarna with Josephine sitting up in the passenger seat.

'Wouldn't it be terrible,' he said, 'if that woman took a liking to me? She'd have nothing to do only break down the wall between the two houses and destroy our peace for ever more.'

All she'd need was reason to knock on his door. If she had reason to knock, he felt sure he'd let her in. If he let her in once she'd be in again and then he'd be in to her and there the trouble would start. One would need a candle and the other would want the lend of a spade. A woman would be a terrible disadvantage: she'd make him match his clothes and take baths. She'd make him drive her to the seaside every fine day with a picnic basket full of bananas and tuna fish sandwiches and ask him where he had gone when he had gone nowhere but into Doolin or down to Ennis for a drop of oil.

December came in wet. Margaret had never known such rain. It didn't come down out of the sky but all skewed, on the wind. There was salt on the windows and a tang of seaweed in the air. People down the town took to drink while the birds went hungry. They played darts for turkeys and hampers, fell out and in again. The women took dead fir trees and holly into their houses, strung multicoloured electric lights under the eaves. Children put pen to paper, sent letters to the North Pole. The postman was run off his feet but Margaret didn't even get a card.

The night before Christmas Eve she walked to the cliffs and back. She had written a few lines to her mother without reply. Her mother could be dead and she wouldn't know. The sea was going mad, eating away the land. By the time she got home, she was soaked. The salt rain made her feel cold and hot at the same time. It was getting dark but there wasn't a light in the parish. The electricity was gone. Margaret threw sods on the fire. The turf hadn't really dried; it smouldered unhappily in the grate, burned away without turning into flame. She longed for wood, big ash sticks she could split with an axe. She imagined herself outside on a fine, frosty morning splitting sticks, stacking them against the wall, and the smell and the heat that would come off them. But sticks were rare in Dunagore. Her mother, who said little, sang Irish:

Cad a dhéanfamid feasta gan adhmad?
Tá deireadh na gcoillte ar lár.

That night, Margaret lit a candle, placed her feet in a basin of soapy water and watched the smouldering turf.

She wondered if the priest had gone to Hell. The priest believed in the afterlife, in God and Heaven and Purgatory, in all of that. He said there wasn't any point believing in Heaven if you didn't believe in Hell. Margaret wondered if she would join him there but it seemed more likely that she'd be turned into a pucán or a dock leaf.

She drank two bottles of stout and felt the past rearing up, all those summers of childish commitment, them saying they'd marry and then him going off and the whole family witnessing his ordination. Him coming back to make hay without so much as a handshake, eating her ribs and parsley sauce and walking alone through the wood beyond the fields. She'd meet him on the stairs, in the cowhouse, on the back lane where the foxgloves turned the ditches pink but he'd pass her with a bare nod same as she was a shadow of what she had been.

And then, one evening, a heavy shower fell out of the blue. The house was sullen; the hay was down.

'That's the end of us,' said her father, standing at the window.

''Tis only a shower.' Her mother, always trying to pacify him.

'Now we will have to buy hay. I said we shouldn't have mowed today. Didn't I say we shouldn't have mowed?' Her father willing the rain to fall harder to prove him right.

'Tomorrow will be fine, surely.'

'What are you saying woman? We're finished.'

Margaret went out in the rain to the wood. She always felt marginally safer when she was outside. The wet Douglas fir looked almost blue. There was the scent of damp fern. Wild anenomes shivered in the damp breeze. She stopped in the clearing where the quickens grew. Their silver boughs shook pleasantly, their leaves trembling. Out in the lane the priest passed, smoking a cigarette, his open-necked shirt wet on the shoulders. The only reason she made her presence known was to ask the simple question of why he never looked her in the eye or asked how she was? Could the man who'd promised her marriage not even ask her how she was? And then she caught up on him and he showed her why. They lay down without a word on the wet grass and she knew while he was planting his seed in her that she would pay for it. Afterwards, he got up and paced between the trees and smoked a cigarette. Then he turned his back and went off without a word.

It was night when Margaret rose. She walked home watching the tops of the trees and, beyond their boughs, the yellow wisp of moon. The experience was like almost everything; it wasn't a patch on what it could have been.

Now she sometimes imagined where she'd be, what she might be doing if she had not made her presence known. She was constantly afraid to take the smallest step in any direction. The greatest lesson the priest had taught her was the lesson of where one step can lead. She stared at the clock above the fire's mantel and came to her senses. The feetwater had grown cold. She dried her feet, cursed a little so she would not cry, and fell asleep in the chair.

When she woke, the fire was almost out and the candle was burnt away to nothing. Outside, no lights flickered in the houses around the coast. The villages of Doolin and Lehinch were still in darkness but the last quarter of that winter moon shone down into her garden. Her neighbour's nanny goat was standing on her hind legs, eating all that was within reach. Margaret hadn't the energy to chase her off. The moon and the clouds looked so still. It was almost Christmas. She dried her feet, went to the priest's bed, and dreamt she was a man.

There was a loft in her dream whose floor sprouted grass. The grass grew higher than a house, its stalks leaning west then east then west again although there was no wind. Margaret lay supine, wearing nothing only a man's trousers and when she put her hand down there, instead of a penis, was a fat lizard which was part of her, the muscular tail swinging back and forth. A woman who looked like herself came in from another century wearing some type of knotted cloth. When she saw the lizard she didn't flinch but took it inside her anyhow and when Margaret woke she felt herself to make sure she wasn't turning into a man. When she saw her hand she got a lovely shock, for she saw blood. She'd thought all that was over. She got up, went into the bathroom and washed herself.

It was almost morning. Grey light framed the trembling curtains. The house was a trap full of draughts. Outside, a gale was blowing. Margaret was used to the wind flattening the long grass in front of her house but it was strange not hearing its power in the trees. She'd never get used to Dunagore, knowing no seed would take root and grow into a sycamore anywhere near that house. She could now smell her own blood. So she was still a child-bearing woman. While she was thinking this she saw the basin of feetwater. She opened the back door and threw it out on the wind. The wind was so loud it shouted like a man.

That same night, at the far side of the wall, Stack couldn't sleep. This often happened. He wondered if other men really slept through the night and woke rested. Some nights he liked being up knowing others were asleep. He would sit at the fire, eating cream buns, watching television with Josephine. Other nights he craved the company of another human being, someone who would be able to change the stations and boil the kettle. He covered

Josephine with his coat. Her hooves were trembling. She dreamt a lot and ate things in her dreams. On fine nights, he sometimes put on his hat and coat and walked the bogs.

That night the electricity failed, he drank five hot whiskeys and thought about the past. Nothing would ever compare to the past: his mother laughing when she noticed him using his left hand; his father teaching him to shave; that summer they all got sunburnt in the bog and took turns with the calamine lotion. How strange it was to hear his father sing and how the song made his mother blush. But his mother and father were dead. He was thinking about death and how he himself would go, when he went, stumbling a little, to Margaret's house. He believed he would die alone and not be found until Josephine ate the door down and somebody recognised her on the road, but death, at least, was certain. Every man needed to be certain of something. It helped to make sense of the day.

He went to Margaret's back door and stood listening. There wasn't a stir. It was getting bright and the sun's light without the sun itself was visible beyond the cliffs. Not a soul knew he was there. He liked being at her door knowing the woman was inside, asleep and safe. He stood for a long time imagining she was his. Then the door opened and Margaret came out, half asleep, with a basin of water, and threw it in his face.

He went home and took his clothes off. Josephine had gone to bed. Beside her, he felt light in the head, was hot in himself then cold. He started to sweat and passed wind. He felt the stone that was always in his throat growing bigger, going down into his stomach. He sat on the toilet for a long time before it passed and when it did it was the size of a stout bottle. When he looked in the mirror, a stranger looked back at him. The stranger was older than he had realised and his lips were parted.

He fell asleep and dreamt of Margaret wearing a bearskin, riding Josephine across the bogs of Clare. Her legs and arms were muscular. He followed Josephine's tracks until she came to the edge of the sea. The woman slapped Josephine hard with a wet leather strap, urging her on into the sea and the pair took off. The waves were high. Stack stood on the edge of the strand, calling out to Josephine to come back: 'Aw, Josie! Come back to me! Josie!' but she got smaller and smaller and in the end he saw Margaret getting down on the coast of Inis Mór and men with red hands surrounding her, leading Josephine by the bridle, taking her away, bribing her with chocolate.

When he woke he felt like a new man. It was eleven o'clock in the night. He had slept through Christmas Eve. It hardly seemed possible but Josephine was standing over him, nipping the soft flesh of his arms. He opened the door and let her out. Margaret Flusk is wild, he thought. Hadn't he seen her bare breast under the fur? Sure didn't she piss outside? Hadn't she got up in her sleep knowing he was there and not so much as blinked when he cried out?

On Christmas morning, he took a bath. He hadn't taken a bath since Halloween. The electricity was still gone. He boiled water on the gas and nearly scalded himself. He polished his shoes, milked Josephine in front of the fire and put a lump of beef into the oven. He didn't know why he was looking at himself or washing himself except it was Christmas and he felt young and strong. If only he hadn't lost his hair. His father, down to the day he was laid in his coffin, had a full head of hair. The undertaker had combed it as he laid him out in the parlour but Stack hadn't cried until the burial was over.

Now he took an eel out of the fridge and put it on the

143

pan to fry. It was a Christmas box from the fishmonger down in Ennistymon who knew Stack had a taste for eel. He was certain it was still good. He looked at the black eel writhing on the pan. It looked alive and, for a moment, he wasn't sure. He bucked himself up, came to his senses and walked up the path to the priest's house.

Margaret wasn't dressed. She was scratching herself and thinking. She liked to roam around in her nightdress having a think, drinking tea in the mornings. She went to the toilet and made sure she was still bleeding. It was strange to be producing eggs again. Wouldn't it be lovely to hatch out eggs like a hen. She had, as a child, followed a hen for days with a hat down over her eyes thinking the hen could not see her but Margaret never found the nest. The hen would lead her astray then disappear through the ferns. Then, out of the blue, she'd walked into the yard with a clutch of eleven chickens.

If only I could cut out the man, Margaret thought, I might have a child. A man was a nuisance and a necessity. If she'd a man she'd have to persuade him to take baths and use his knife and fork. She ripped a towel in two and made herself a sanitary towel, scalded the pot and waited for the tea to draw. Beyond the pane, standing there in his shirtsleeves staring at her, was the bachelor from next door. She wanted to stand there and stare him down but it was Christmas and, out of common decency, she opened the door. The bachelor looked clean but there was a strange smell off him.

'Stack's my name.'

'Stack?' What kind of a name was that?

'I'm your neighbour,' he said, gesturing to his own house.

'Is that so?'

144

'Some Christmas, and you with no electric to make a bit of dinner.'

'What matter.'

'Come in and have your breakfast. I've gas.'

'You've gas!' Margaret laughed.

'Aye.'

'I'm not hungry.'

'You're not hungry. Well, that's a good one. Don't you know the moon is changing?'

'The moon?' Margaret said. What did he know about the moon?

'Put on your sheepskin, good woman,' he said. 'Hurry on. The fry will be in cinders.'

She didn't think. She got the sheepskin and her boots and followed him down the path to her front gate which was opening and closing on its hinges. There were goat droppings all over his front yard. His porch was full of bicycle parts and the cab of a tractor and the kitchen darker than the sea. In the gas light she saw spades and shovels cocked up against the chimney wall and, hanging from the central beam, a scythe. A live snake was being fried in a pool of oil. On the table thick cuts of brown bread and a tub of fake butter. Margaret, in nothing only her nightdress and her coat, felt lovelier than the raven. I'm producing eggs, she thought. I'm bleeding. I'm past nothing. Let this day bring what it will.

Stack held a bag of defrosted peas up to the candle to read the cooking directions.

'I better cook these so they'll not go to waste.'

Margaret could read the directions from where she sat. Maybe he was going blind. And the things he kept: seashells, a calendar from 1985, bottle tops, dead batteries, pictures of dead popes. There was a picture of Stack when he was about twenty with a full head of hair, three Sacred Heart pictures, barometers, and inside the window, behind the television, a fan to keep the window pane from fogging up. So, he likes to know who's walking the roads, she thought. Through an open door, she saw a big, unmade bed. She could smell the goat. Maybe the goat slept with him. Just imagine.

'Don't mind the house,' he said. 'I've no woman.'

'No?'

'Well, I had a woman one time and now I'm not sorry I don't have her. She was a fierce expense.'

'Maybe you should find yourself a woman with money.'

'If a woman had money, she wouldn't want me.'

'Why, have you a wooden leg?'

He laughed. It was a queer sort of laugh, closer to sadness than amusement. For a moment, she imagined his life and felt for him. Did anyone ever know what another was going through?

'No, thank God. And by the looks of you, your legs aren't wooden either.' He was putting the two of them together, adding them up in his mind.

'You must have left school early,' Margaret said.

'Why's that?'

'It gets more complicated after you learn to add.'

'What?' he said. 'Oh, your tongue is quick.'

When he said the word she was back again under the quicken trees. Neither she nor the priest could help themselves. She felt him on top of her, panting, rolling over onto his stomach, zipping himself up, ashamed. And the thrill of it: the thrill after a decade of sitting on ricks of hay, eating scallions, him leaving the first primrose on the saddle of her bike. By breaking his vows of celibacy it felt possible that he might, somehow, make others. There was blood that night too. Beyond his head she could see the bright orange berries of the quicken trees.

'Josephine is minded better nor any woman in Ireland,' Stack was saying, nodding in the direction of the armchair.

There, in the dark, was the nanny goat staring at her. Her eyes were frightening. Stack reached up and took a sprig of holly from behind a picture. Margaret thought he was going to give it to her but he gave it to Josephine, who ate it.

'What part of the country did you come from?' he said.

'Wicklow.'

'The goat-suckers,' he said. 'That explains it.'

'Did you ask me in to insult me?'

'That wouldn't be hard, you're proud,' he said, prodding the eel with a fork. 'This is ready. Pull up a chair.'

She didn't want to pull up a chair, didn't want to sit in that awful place eating fried snake with all those dead people on the walls. Well, what did she expect? What happens when a woman follows a man into his house wearing little more than her nightdress on Christmas morning? But she was smelling burnt flesh and toast, watching the teapot steam. She hadn't eaten yesterday. It is the stomach, not the heart, that drives us, she thought. She was grateful the room was dark so she couldn't see the extent of the dirt and could eat in ignorance. Josephine sat under the table with her own buttered toast.

'Most people have dogs,' Margaret said.

'Ah but the goat!' Stack said, starting off on his favourite subject. 'The goat is a great advantage. She'll eat anything. She'll go anywhere. She's twice the size of any dog, she's like a radiator going around heating the place and, to top it all, I've milk. Do you like goat's milk?'

'No. But they say it's a noble child that's baptised in it.'

'Do they now?' He was looking into the oven at the beef. It had begun to spit and he lowered the flame. 'Are you one of these superstitious women?'

Her mouth was so full she couldn't answer. The eel was lovely. Once, her mother took her out to eat in the mart. Big dinners were cheap there. A neighbour came in and ordered his plate. He was white in the face. Her mother watched him getting his dinner and going off to a corner with his back to all his neighbours and said, 'Do you see that man there? If you ever see a man like that, leave him alone till he's had his fill. A man like that is dangerous.' Margaret now felt like that man. She drank the tea, ate several cuts of toast and most of the eel.

Stack looked at her big nose and her long hair and filled her cup again. He cut more eel and watched her. While she ate he could not help wondering what a child they'd have together would look like.

'Do you not miss your own part of the country?'

'I miss the trees,' she said. 'I miss the ash.'

The quicken tree, the mountain ash, were all the one.

'Well, you can't be blamed for that,' he said. 'There's no fire like an ash fire.'

Margaret swallowed the last of what she had and looked at him. She looked at his grey eyes. He seemed decent and why should she mind that he was odd? All the finest people she'd known were odd.

Stack bantered on. He criticised young people and turf, the Taoiseach, talked about New Year's resolutions and sunburn. When he stopped to draw breath, Margaret went home.

He's a lonely man, she thought, and he's desperate. But that goat! She'd have no time for that goat, sitting up like a witch in the dark.

When Margaret reached her own house, the door was wide open and a litter of black mongrel pups was running across the floor. They'd chewed the corners off her library books, got up on every stick of furniture and left dirty paw marks all over her lovely white bedspread. One black pup trotted over, licked her hand and wagged its tail. She turned him up and saw, under his belly, a penis. She threw him out and thought about Stack. She couldn't understand why she'd followed a total stranger into his house and eaten all that food when it could be poisoned. She could still see the big bald head and him reaching up for the sprig of holly.

That night she saw children rounding up the pups, whistling, flashlights shining, green eyes racing like demons in all directions. There were dogs in the graveyard the night she walked all over the priest's grave. So, they were back. The priest was jealous but the priest was dead. She felt an awful chill and pulled a cardigan over her nightdress. She had no way of boiling the kettle for a hot water bottle. She sat in the candlelight until the candle was burnt out. Then she groped her way into the bedroom and lay there in the darkness knowing now what was on the far side of the wall.

When the pubs opened after Christmas, there was talk. The Flusk woman was seen coming out of Stack's in nothing only a nightdress. He must have sheared her, they said, because there was no sign of the sheepskin. Stack carried her across his own yard and into her own house. Some said it stopped there.

'He must be drinking his Bovril, so,' said the grocer.

'Sure wouldn't he need a stepladder just to reach her knickers?'

'Ah, we're all the same height lying down,' said an old man.

'Imagine the two of 'em wudout a stitch,' said the draper's wife. 'They'd frighten one another.'

'Not half as big a fright as she'd get,' said the auctioneer who was doing his best to join in but was in a terrible way with a toothache.

'You mean a small fright,' said the barmaid who was single and getting older and pretending not to care. 'Two hailstones and a mouse's tail.'

'You should know,' they all said because they knew the barmaid thought that would be a nice cosy little number up there in the cottage with Stack, looking down on all the tourists in the summertime and him with plenty of money and nobody to spend it on only herself and Josephine.

In Dunagore the smoke kept rising. Margaret bought two boxes of sanitary towels in the supermarket and set the women talking.

'There could be a babby in Dunagore yet!'

'Wouldn't Stack be the proud father?'

'Sure isn't the spring coming?'

Margaret walked between the showers, kept track of her eggs and the changing moon. Daylight lasted longer but towards evening the red sun always sank into the sea. Dirty suds floated up on the edge of the strand. The heather was thick, took on new growth like hair all over the boglands. Tourists wandered into Doolin looking for Irish music and mussels, directions to holy wells. Men came down from Dublin to test themselves on the golf course at Lehinch, lost balls and found others. A hitchhiker knocked on Margaret's door and asked in a german accent which way was east. Margaret pointed towards home and the young woman took off over the fields.

On Valentine's Day, she went outside and there, at the front door, was a load of ash sticks. Stack had left them during the night. He'd made a phone call while he was drunk, gone up to Limerick and traded two lorry-loads of turf for the load of sticks.

Margaret got in the car and took off down the road to Ennistymon. She met but could not avoid another car on the narrow road. They both lost their side mirrors, stopped, shrugged and went on again. When she got to the town the man on the bridge signalled her to stop:

'Seven cabbages for a pound!'

People were buying cards, red roses. Margaret bought an axe, came back and spent the morning splitting the ash. That night she built an almighty fire. She sat at the hearth with her feet in the basin, sweating. She drank the sherry she'd bought for a trifle she never made and thought about her son. He would be nine years old, if he was alive. She'd heard the banshee the evening before he died but mistook her for a stray cat. The child was fast asleep in the cot that night. He was such a deep sleeper, it made her nervous. Sometimes she put her hand near his mouth to make sure he was still breathing. She had placed her hand near his mouth several times that night and the next morning he was cold, the tinge of blue on his lips. She stopped the clock and ran up the wood with him in her arms. She stayed there all night but in the end came home to face it all.

'Cot death,' the doctor said. 'It happens.'

She would never forgive him for that. In any case, she wasn't the type to forgive; forgiving might mean forgetting and she preferred to hold onto her bitterness, and her memory. But always she blamed herself.

Shortly after his birth, a fisherman from Rosslare came to see her.

'I hear you've kept the child's caul,' he said. 'I'll give you me last penny for it. Me father and the one brother I had on this earth drowned.'

'I couldn't sell it.'

'If you let me buy that caul, I'll be safe at sea.'

'Not for love nor money will I sell it.'

'Well, money is all I can offer,' he'd said, and went away.

She knew it wasn't right to refuse him but she could not bear to part with it. And then the child died and in the end she'd thrown the caul on the fire. What upset her most was the little things he'd never done; to think he'd never taken a step nor climbed a tree nor witnessed a wet summer. She had taken for granted a future of homework on the kitchen table, exercise books marked with gold and silver stars, a mucky hurl inside the front door, measuring his shoulders for a blazer. And then the future was blotted out, gone, like something that falls from sight without a sound.

February turned into a March of many weathers. Margaret's superstition deepened. When she stopped at the pub in Doolin for a bowl of soup and saw a cat sitting with her back to the fire she ran out and ordered more coal. Always the hills looked closer or black before it rained. One morning she woke and saw a crow sitting on top of the wardrobe. She drove to the chapel and lit a candle for the soul of her child. It was the first time she had gone to the chapel. An old woman was kneeling outside the confession box. Margaret lit a candle at the feet of Saint Anthony, knelt in the front pew and stared at the ambo. She imagined the priest standing there giving out sermons while her belly got bigger with his child. She had not intended to pray but when she looked up her knees were sore, the woman was gone, and children were rehearsing their First Communion. She watched each boy, looked for the face of a child she'd never see, filled her sherry bottle from the font in the porch and walked across the square.

A caravan was parked beside the vegetable stand. *Meet Madame Nowlan, Teller of the Future*, the sign read. Margaret went on down to the hotel and ordered a fried herring. Outside, the crows seemed anxious. When she finished eating she wanted a drink but she did not really know what to ask for. They had kept whiskey at home for sick calves, and poteen to rub on greyhounds but nobody ever drank anything except stout at Christmas or for when the hay was saved. People seldom came to their house but when they did, they drank the calves' whiskey and her father complained afterwards that he'd have to go out and buy more.

She walked over to the bar and pointed at a bottle. Sambuca was written on the label. She asked for a large. The barman asked her if she wanted it straight and she said yes, thinking this might be some kind of glass. It tasted like liquorice and took away the aftertaste of the herring. People came in looking at her. She could read their minds. There's the woman who had the priest's child. There's the woman who lives on her own. There's that Flusk woman Stack's after. When she couldn't stand it any more, she got up and walked back to the caravan.

Reluctantly she stepped up into the candlelight. Madame Nowlan was eating a rock bun, pulling raisins out of the dough with her fingernails. She had blonde hair and a fake tan. A pot of tea was left out on the table.

'You want your fortune told, love?'

'I'm not sure.'

'Come on in. There's no harm.' On her radio, Willie Nelson was singing a song about loving someone in his own peculiar way. 'I'll read your leaves.'

Margaret drank the tea and they talked for a while about

the weather. The woman was an expert on rain. It felt strange to talk to another human being. She hadn't held a conversation since Christmas and found it a terrible effort, trying to make sense of another's words, then her own and all the possibilities for misunderstanding that went on in between. Madame Nowlan pulled out a mirror and drew lipstick across her mouth.

'How do I look?'

'You look fine.'

Then she picked up Margaret's cup and casually began to read the leaves.

'I see a dead child by a local man. I see property, a house up on a hill, and terrible shame. There's no need for this shame. It wasn't your fault the child died. I see the number seven and a man with an S in his name. You already know this man. There's trees in your memory. You're mule stubborn. Don't stay in the place you're in. There's a shadow on the back of that house. You must rear your next child in the Irish tongue. Who is this goat? There's a jealousy here I can't understand.'

'My neighbour has a goat.'

'It's unhealthy, this goat. Well, you've lost and gained your fertility. That much is clear. Why are your people so hard? They turned their backs on you over this religious man. Have another child,' she said. 'The time is now. The next child will make your life worth living. After him, you'll stop looking down over the cliffs. But give the next sea-man his caul. The last man you refused drowned.'

'He did not.'

The woman was silent now.

'That's terrible,' said Margaret, looking at her feet.

'Is there anything you'd like to ask?'

She couldn't speak for a while. Eventually she said, 'Do

you see anything about my mother?'

'Your mother? Your mother is gone to a better place.'

Margaret thanked her and gave her whatever was in her pocket. Driving back, the roads looked steeper, the hedges taller. The ponies seemed enormous. It took her several minutes to get the key in the lock and when she did she stripped and sat in front of the fire. She lay down on the floor not realising, until she tasted salt, that she was crying. She began to wail. Stack heard her grief floating through the stone wall.

A few hours later she was out again, naked but for the big sheepskin and her leather boots, walking the road to the cliffs. Stack followed her but his legs were not as long as hers, and he did not catch up until she stopped at Moher. She was down on her belly in the wet grass looking over the precipice. Ages passed. It was getting darker. Stack kept well away but stared at the back of her neck until she turned and faced him. She looked wild but her voice was calm.

'I was in love with him,' she said simply.

'Don't I know.'

'I lost his child. Look.' She opened two buttons and showed him her caesarean scar.

'That must have been awful.'

'It was,' she said. 'It was terrible.'

Waves kept forming on the surface of the ocean. The wind wasn't blowing hard but neither would it stop. Neither one of them wanted anything to stop. Stack wished he had a full head of hair. He wished he hadn't wasted all those years on the farmer's daughter.

'I've never been in love,' he said. 'I've nobody only Josephine.'

'That would break my heart.'

He turned to look at her. 'Your heart's already broken.'

As soon as he said this, her opinion of him rose. She looked back at the ocean. It wasn't angry. Each wave seemed to brake before the cliffs, slowing before the end of its journey and yet the next waves kept on as though they had learned nothing from the ones that went before.

'You must think it strange, me telling you these things.'

'I suppose I do. But I doubt I'll ever understand women. Tell me this: what sort of woman pisses outside?'

Margaret laughed. She pushed her head and shoulders out over the Atlantic and let her laughter fall. She was not daunted by the ocean or the height of the cliffs. While her laughter fell, Stack realised he was more than half afraid of her.

'Come on,' he said. 'It's getting dark.'

They headed for home. They had said so much that they were now at a loss for what next to say. A few council workers were finishing up for the day, spreading the last of the hot tar.

'God bless the work,' said Margaret.

The labourer looked up at her and tipped his hat.

From a distance the two houses on the Hill of Dunagore looked like one, with Margaret's smoke whirling around the lighted windows. Stack, not wanting the walk to end, slowed down on the hill but Margaret did not alter her pace to suit him. She walked on, her bare legs mounting the hill, her hair blowing wild around her head. When she reached Dunagore she didn't even bid him goodnight but walked into her own house and shut the door.

Summer came and the rain eased off. Swallows flew back and found their nests, woodbine climbed the ditches and the heather bloomed. A stranger knocked on Margaret's door one Tuesday morning, a dark-haired man with a troubled look.

'I hear,' he said, 'that you can cure a toothache.'

Margaret wasn't surprised. 'Are you in a bad way?'

'I'm demented.' He sat down and covered his face with his hands and started to cry.

Margaret went outside and caught a frog.

'Put her back legs in your mouth without harming her and the pain will go,' she said. 'If you harm her the pain will double.'

He held the frog. 'Put her back legs in me mouth?'

'Yes.'

'Well,' he said. 'I'll try anything.'

'How did you find out about me?'

'The Nowlan woman in the caravan told me. She says you're a seventh child, that you have the cure.'

He went out with the frog and four days later she got the first letter she ever got in Dunagore.

Dear Miss Flusk,

I don't know myself. No pain since the morning after I saw you and the frog has taken up residence near the rain barrel. Many thanks,

John McCarthy,
auctioneer

That evening a load of birch was delivered to her door.

'What's all this?' said Margaret.

'I dunno,' said the fellow on the lorry. 'It's from the man with the toothache. That's all I know.'

Soon the whole parish started to come. There were men with boils and women who wanted no more children;

157

women who were desperate for children, and a child that was born on Christmas Day who saw ghosts and couldn't eat. They had shingles and gout and stones in their throats, bad knees and haunted cow-houses. Margaret placed her hands on these strangers and felt their fears and their fears put her heart crossways. The people left in good faith and their ailments and their apparitions disappeared. She'd wake and find new spuds and rhubarb and pots of jam and bags of apples and sticks outside her back door. Her dreams grew black as the charred doors of Hell. She started to tell God she was sorry, started sleeping late and when she woke, neighbouring women would be there frying rashers, boiling eggs, talking. Strange men came and cleaned the moss off her roof, put new hinges on the gate, new putty in the windows.

Margaret grew frightened of her own death and passed water all around the house after dark. This still gave her satisfaction. One night, after a rich man asked if she could turn his old friend into a sow, she couldn't help herself. She went in to tell Stack. When they stopped laughing, Stack thought of her slapping Josephine with the leather strap and the strange island men leading her away. The men in his dream outnumbered him. That was the hardest part of the dream. He suddenly knew she'd move away and couldn't bear the thought of her being gone. She had taken off her boots and was there rubbing her feet in his kitchen. Her feet were bigger than shoe-boxes and reminded him of a song.

'You've a fine pair of feet,' he said, 'God bless them.'

She didn't answer; she just kept the silence and sat looking at him. He looked strong from the bogs. There were clocks, too many clocks ticking on his walls. She realised she hadn't wound her clock in weeks, as though that could stop time. She didn't want time to stop but the strangers were always coming, their palms filled with hatred and bitterness and even though she didn't know half their names, it was all contagious. She thought about the Nowlan woman and what she'd said about the child.

'My eggs are right.'

'Your eggs?'

'Come to bed for an hour.'

When they went into the bedroom Josephine was under the quilt. Margaret laughed while Stack tried to lift her. When he unbuttoned himself and she saw his penis, she thought of the lizard in her dream. He hadn't, at first, a notion what to do but nature took over. Josephine did her best to get between them. When Margaret woke, Stack was gone and the goat was staring at her. There was a terrible stink of goat and hair all over the bed.

Margaret went back to her own house and ate two tins of red salmon, skin, bones and all and washed it down with a pint of buttermilk. She looked in the mirror. The whites of her eyes were like snow and her skin had turned into the skin of a woman who lives in salt wind.

The next morning she went into Stack's house. He hadn't slept, had walked the bogs half the night with Josephine.

'Do you have a sledgehammer?' she said.

'No,' he said.

'No?'

'But I've a fair idea what you're thinking.'

'You have?'

'I've been thinking meself.'

'Do you mind?'

'I don't,' he said. 'Isn't it the sensible thing to do? But I should be the one to do it.'

'No,' she said.

159

Margaret drove to Ennistymon and bought the sledge. As she drove along, she wondered what the priest would think. He would look at her mortal frame walking around his house, having conceived another illegitimate child. He would still be regretting the day he ever laid a hand on her but it was his weakness as much as his destiny that made him stretch out his hand. He was ten years older than her and it was him, not her, who had broken his vows to the Lord. And hadn't she paid for her side with the death of the child? And that wasn't her fault. Hadn't the gypsy woman said it wasn't her fault?

When she got to Ennistymon, the mad man on the bridge signalled her to stop.

'There's ostriches on the road!' he cried. 'Slow down!'

She was glad there were crazy people in the world. She watched him, wondering if she wasn't herself a bit mad. When she rounded the corner, ostriches were walking down the main street. People were standing on the footpaths watching them go past and a young girl with plaited hair was driving them along with a stick. So, being mad was the same as having your wits about you, Margaret thought. Sometimes everybody was right. For most of the time people crazy or sober were stumbling in the dark, reaching with outstretched hands for something they didn't even know they wanted.

She was expecting a child. She knew this the way she knew, after Christmas morning, that it was Stack, not the wind, on her doorstep; it was him shouted.

Margaret came home, pulled the priest's bed out of the room, took it down the field, and set fire to it. It was slow to burn at first, then blazed and turned into a bed of ash. She went inside and began to knock a hole in the wall between the two houses. Stack stood in his own house at the dividing wall and felt afraid. When that wall came down nothing again would ever be the same. He could feel the grief of Margaret Flusk. Her grief was beyond comparison. And her strength; Margaret had the strength of two men. Weren't her legs and arms the same as in his dream? He stood there and heard the plaster loosen, then the stones.

She was there half the day. When she saw light at the other side it reminded her of the time her mother woke her, as a child, on Easter morning so she could see the sun dancing, to witness the resurrection of Christ. When she got through the hole in the wall, Stack was singing.

'They say Clare people are musical,' she said.

'They say Wicklow people suck goats' milk from the teat.'

'That's why we're so good-looking.'

'You're a quare woman.'

'Do you think this child will live?'

'I don't know.'

'Do you know nothing?' she said.

'No.'

'Neither do I.'

'Aren't we blessed?'

Josephine did not like the new arrangement. Stack did not seem to love her any more. He didn't even warm his hands before he milked her and he forgot to rub Palmolive on her teats. The woman stole her milk, tied her to his bedpost, then told Stack she belonged in the shed. When Josephine gave birth, Margaret weaned her kid just as early as she could and took her off on a rope to an ugly-looking pucán over the hill.

Stack had never eaten as well. Margaret churned butter, baked bread, made cheese out of Josephine's milk and spent the rest of her days eating chocolate. He couldn't keep her in chocolate. It was like throwing biscuits to Josephine. He'd go down to the shop and come home with Mars bars and Maltesers and find she'd taken another one of his mother's possessions down the field and set fire to it. She was always lighting fires, going around with a big belly bumping into things and then running outside to throw up her food. And always she went to piss outside after dark.

Day and night, the whole parish came: every man, woman and child, looking to get rid of ghosts and ring-worm. The kettle was always boiling, teapots going and poor Josephine tied up, imprisoned in the shed. Even the priest came, saying he had a bad leg and was there any-thing Margaret could do for him?

Margaret could tell what Stack was thinking, beat him at cards and split a load of sticks while he'd be thinking about it. She threw out the television, wouldn't let him have holly in the house at Christmas, and watched him when he ate. And at night she kept herself well clear of him, was as bad as the small farmer's daughter who, in fairness, never threw up her dinners.

They say something bad will happen if you don't throw out the feetwater. They say man should not live alone. They say if you see a goat eating dock leaves, it will rain. Margaret gave birth in the priest's house. There were thir-teen women and nine children there that day running around with scissors and boiling water and telling Stack to get out of the way. He sat in his own side of the house with Josephine. Margaret's screams shook the parish. Stack

162

imagined he heard a slap and the cry of a child for several hours before he heard them and then an old woman's voice saying, '. . . easy knowing it isn't her first.'

Now that Stack knew a woman, there grew the knowledge that he would never understand women. They could smell rain, read doctors' handwriting, hear the grass growing.

Margaret christened her son Michael, baptised him with a jugful of Josephine's milk. When a fisherman came over from Inis Mór to buy the caul she would not take a penny. She invited him in and treated him like royalty, made him sherry trifle and custard. They talked late into the night until Stack grew tired and went to bed. When he woke, Margaret was still in the chair and Michael was fast asleep in the fisherman's arms.

By that time the two houses were clean as polished wood. The two chimneys that had poured out smoke onto the Hill of Dunagore were now one. Wood and turf leant against their gable walls. The opening the woman had torn down was framed in wood and had hinges which were attached to a door which opened and sometimes closed. Stack looked younger. Somebody saw him in Ennis having a shave, sitting up in the barber's chair with a towel around his shoulders, telling a dirty joke.

Margaret did her best to give up on superstition. She started to believe that nothing she didn't believe in could harm her. But however she changed her behaviour, she could do nothing about her nature. In all the years she lived in Dunagore, she never lit her own fire, never failed to pull rushes in February and, hard as she tried, could never throw out ashes on a Monday or go out as far as the clothesline without placing the tongs across the pram.

If, on the occasional dark night, she thought about the

priest she did not dwell on it. The Lord's work was indeed mysterious. If she hadn't lost the priest's child, she would not have inherited his house. If she hadn't inherited his house, she would not have been washing her feet that night, and she might have remembered to throw out the feetwater instead of throwing it like a spell over Stack and eaten his Christmas snake and had his child. As it stood, she had got into that bed beside the goat. And you know what they say about goats: it is said that goats can see the wind. Margaret too could see the wind; in her dreams she saw it shake the quicken trees, how the berries changed into beads of blood which fell on the grass all around that place where she had lain.

As for the child, he was nothing like Stack. For years he waited to see some mark of himself in his own son but none came. It mystified without surprising him. It was as though Margaret had spit the child or hatched him. As a mother she was ferocious. Stack saw her bare her teeth at neighbours who stroked the child's hair. And she gave him his own way at every turn. During his infancy, she rocked him until she had him ruined. Stack hardly got a wink of sleep. Margaret didn't seem to need sleep. She'd be up at dawn and up every five minutes to check the child was breathing, then fall back into dreams which made her kick him, and often he got up and went back to his old bed.

Michael never crawled. He got out of his chair one day and made it all the way to the front gate and back. One day Stack went in to milk Josephine and found there wasn't a drop of milk in her teats for the boy had sucked her dry. When the boy got hardy he went around the bogs with Stack, jumping ditches with a pole, wading in bog-water and was never sick a day in his life. He'd eat nothing only fish fingers, turnips and sweet things, rode Josephine around the front lawn, bought ducks and pushed them around the narrow roads of Dunagore in his own pram and grew tall as a stake. He could write his name backwards and upside-down. He made up stories, told lies when he was bored and walked around the house in his sleep. Margaret wouldn't let him go to school, said there was nothing the people of that parish could teach him that she couldn't teach better.

Michael was seven before Margaret gave up on the parishioners' ailments and apparitions. She'd had enough of them and knew, if she sent her child to school, that he would suffer. But it was a long time before the people of Clare gave up hope and stopped leaving jam and sticks and herrings for Margaret Flusk and started doing her harm. One morning she got up and found peacock feathers stuffed through the letter-box. On another morning, all her tyres were flat. She herself could withstand anything but her fears hovered round the child.

Stack knew she was going before she went. She let the fire die one night, and the following morning Stack found himself walking down to the edge of the strand. He wanted to be there when it happened. He stood at the water's edge and stared west. The day was calm. Soon a fishing boat full of Island men came into Doolin and a boat was lowered into the sea. The strangers rowed slowly to shore, their oars cutting neatly into the salt water. When they reached the land they tipped their caps but did not speak. One man looked familiar. When Stack turned, Margaret was looking him straight in the face then wading out, climbing without a word into the boat. The boy cried but Stack knew he would not cry for long. He held his son in his arms then let him go.

The morning was fine, the sea glassy. Nothing stopped him from getting on board, nothing at all. For a moment the men waited and it seemed that all he had to do to make his future happy was to climb into that boat and be carried away on a tide cut by the strength of other men. Instead Stack stood on the strand and watched the only woman he had ever loved vanish from sight. It didn't take long. Closer to the shore a pair of gulls screeched over the water as though there was something down there only they could see. Stack watched them until his eyes grew sore then he climbed back up the hill.

When he got home, he let Josephine off the rope and soon she had her forelegs on the table, eating all that was left of a rhubarb tart. The track of Margaret's thumbs was baked into the edge of the pastry. He was glad of Josephine. He could at least fulfil her needs. He sat down and looked for a long time at the bare, clean rooms. The sun shone on the teapot's lid, the linoleum, the polished wood. So Margaret was gone. Hadn't he always known she'd go? Hadn't the dream told him? But he couldn't judge her, not even when she took his son's hand and rowed away with strangers. They were, after all, divided by nothing but a strip of deep salt water which he could easily cross.

Josephine licked the plate clean and stared at Stack. He followed her into their old bedroom, shut the door and closed his eyes. Tomorrow he would go down to Doolin and buy a bag of cement and brick up that wall. He would buy a bottle of whiskey, some fig rolls, and leave the television in to be repaired. He would not be idle. Winter was coming. The turf would keep him busy, and fit. There'd be long winter nights and storms to blot out and remind him of the past. Although he was no longer young his near future was a certainty. But if he lived for a hundred years, he would never again venture up to a woman's house in the night nor let her come anywhere near him with feetwater.

Some notes on the folklore/stories

The quicken tree is another name for the mountain ash or the rowan tree. It is believed to be a tree of formidable magical and protective powers. It is mentioned in mythology as having the power of enchantment. The Irish name, *caorthann*, derives from the word *caor* which means both a berry and a blazing flame. The name 'quicken' refers to its quickening or lifegiving powers.

Lisdoonvarna is a small town in County Clare famous for its match-making festival.

A crannóg is an early Irish dwelling.

The words of the mother's song: 'What will we do for timber now that the woods are gone?'

A pucán is a sexually active male goat.

Inis Mór is the largest and most western of the Aran Islands.

Wicklow people are nicknamed goatsuckers.

A garsún is a young boy.

Poteen is an Irish spirit equivalent to moonshine.

Placing the tongs across the pram is said to prevent fairies from stealing the child and leaving a changeling in its place.

'Surrender' was inspired by an incident recollected in John McGahern's *Memoir*, concerning his father who sat on a bench in Galway and ate twenty-four oranges before he married.

Acknowledgements

The author most gratefully acknowledges the assistance of The Arts Council of Ireland, The Society of Authors and The Harold Hyam Wingate Foundation in London.

Thanks also to The Tyrone Guthrie Centre at Annaghmakerrig and The Blue Mountain Centre in Upstate New York. To Brian Leyden for the Leitrim names; Viv McDade, James Ryan and my editors Angus Cargill and Joan Bingham at Grove, for their insightful criticism and to Gerald Dawe, Ian Jack and Fatema Ahmed for suggesting titles.

The author would also like to acknowledge the work and care of students and staff while resident at Dublin City University, University College, Cork and University College, Dublin. Special thanks to David Marcus, Colm Tóibín and Declan Kiberd for their generous encouragement and support.

An earlier version of 'Close to the Water's Edge' was published in *Birthday Stories*, The Harvill Press, selected and edited by Haruki Murakami.

'Night of the Quicken Trees' was published in *Arrows in Flight*, Scribner/Townhouse, edited by Caroline Walsh.

'Dark Horses' won The Francis MacManus Award, 2005; it was subsequently broadcast on RTE, Radio One and published in *These Are Our Lives*, The Stinging Fly Press, edited by Declan Meade.

'The Forester's Daughter' was published in *The Faber Book of Best New Irish Stories 2004-2005*, edited by David Marcus.

'The Parting Gift' was published in *Granta 94: Loved Ones*.